THE VORT PROGRAMME

By the same author

John Rankine

THE VORT PROGRAMME

LONDON : DENNIS DOBSON

First published in Great Britain 1979 by
Dobson Books Ltd., 80 Kensington Church Street, London W8

Photoset by
Bristol Typesetting Co. Ltd.,
Barton Manor, St. Philips, Bristol
Printed and bound in Great Britain by
William Clowes & Sons Ltd, Beccles and London

ISBN 0234 72112 X

CHAPTER ONE

Cain's shuttle broke through low ceiling cloud and the Western Region terminal was spread out nearer than he thought. There was the river and high rise waterfront development on either bank, yellow-green flatland, and the port itself with a facility vehicle dwarfing the flight control block as it crawled out to a launch pad.

There was nothing to do to keep his mind on load. The console had broken out into a rash of green lights as the auto pilot locked on to a docking beam to bring him in.

He fished in a pocket of his bush jacket and brought out a stubby briar pipe, filled it with pleasurable care and had wreathed his head in aromatic blue smoke when the shuttle planed to a meticulous landfall fifty metres from the reception concourse.

The scanner glowed with a head and shoulders picture of a brunette in a silly hat and a set smile. A cosy voice said 'Welcome to Picton City Space Port. Please place your identity folder in the viewer.'

Except for the pipe, she had a reasonable match with the face looking at her over the unfolded oblong. Medium brown hair, short, well-trimmed beard, zig-zag scar on the left temple, creases round the eyes which were pale blue and unblinking.

Proving that she could read as well as the next girl, she picked up his name from the manifest and used it. 'Mr Cain. Science Correspondent with Southern Actualities.'

'That's right.'

'What will be the length of your visit?'

'Why? What do you have in mind?'

The smile lost a little of its warmth. She had gotten another joker in the lottery and it was tough at the end of a long stint. 'You know the regulation. If it is to be more than a week we are required to inform Public Safety.'

'Ah. You disappoint me. Longer than a week. I shall be enrolling at Picton Polytech. Public Safety will pick up the reference from there.'

'Very well. You have permission to leave your car.'

'Thank you very much.'

'You are welcome.'

A trolley with an android operator was coming across the apron to take care of his gear. He shoved back the hatch and climbed out.

Cooler here. A small damp breeze bringing a smell of the sea. The last of the April sun dropping behind the city skyline.

It was all new. But so many places had been new. In a month it would be all one. Familiar and unfamiliar; so many rooms so many streets, so many casual contacts.

The android detached itself from its trolley, stubbed a lever on the skin of the car and the panel of the freight bay slid aside. Grabs hooked on to a small cabin trunk and swung it out.

Cain walked beside it, up a ramp into reception across the busy floor and out again through a check point to the dispersal bay.

A blue and yellow auto car peeled off the stick above and dropped towards him.

It was all routine. He could have been coming in to any major city in the Atlantic Federation.

But there was a difference and the nudge of a sixth sense brought it up loud and clear as the car swept a metre over the landing strip and was practically vertical overhead.

An adrenalin boost got him off to a spring start and he

6

dived in a compact forward roll which brought him up against one of the support columns of the porch.

The car dropped eight metres in free fall and its undercarriage crumpled on the parquet. The next car in line left the rank, rose into the Metropolitan throughway and shot off towards the city. An alarm siren started a frenetic bleep.

The porch had filled up like a sluice and two port security details in dark blue uniforms used carbine butts to shove a path through the ring around the wreck. A deep chested, matronly type on the front row said with satisfaction. 'I saw it all. He was a big, burly man with a gingery beard. I was just saying to my friend that I couldn't ever go for a man with a beard. They never look *clean*. And she said, she reckoned anybody with a beard had something to hide like a weak chin or a facial blemish and then this car came right in under the roof and fell right on him. I guess he'll be crushed as flat as a pancake.'

It was clear that she rated it as one of the hazards of going about with facial hair.

Cain left his pillar and pushed into the circle. It was an unpopular move because those early at the wake reckoned they had their rights. But there was some recognition that he had a case when the woman notched her voice into an awed squeak and said. 'It's him. It's his spirit,' and fell back dramatically into the arms of her friend.

Cain said, 'Some malfunction, Officer. Power failure, I'd guess. It was coming in, overshot the driveway and fell.'

'Do you want to make a complaint?'

That was a difficult one. Either way it was awkward. Saying no would look eccentric, saying yes would mean time spent at an enquiry and press coverage.

The set lit with a bright flash and the woman who had swum back woozily out of her vapours took it as another occult phenomenon and gave a nervous scream.

So the die was already cast. He said, 'Of course I shall

make a complaint. I could have been killed. I'd be glad if you'd have that wreck lifted away and then I could see what damage has been done to my gear.'

The second guard was dispersing the crowd. They were ready to go. It was a let down. The man was not even scratched and likely to get a fat compensation fee out of it. Nothing was the same as it was. You couldn't even rely on a straightforward accident.

In the Controller's office, Cain reconciled himself to another mug shot and even said a piece for the record. He confessed that his immediate reaction had been one of surprise and that he was glad to have escaped unhurt. He revealed that he was on his way to Picton Polytech and that in spite of all he liked his first impression of the city and was looking forward to his stay.

It was the minimum, but he knew nobody was going to be pleased.

Welcome at the coal face of culture was more restrained. The auto car dropped him at street level before an imposing granite ziggurat on a plateau, and his trunk dropped through a delivery trap onto a gravity conveyor and went its own way. He walked up twenty-three steps, crossed a colonnaded porch and pushed through a revolving door to a round circulation space with a horseshoe reception desk in the centre.

A clerk with a high balding forehead and long narrow hands took his identity folder and set it on a scanner, saying 'You are late Mr Cain. We expect registration before 1600. You will only just have time to complete the circuit.

'Then the sooner you finish your part of the business the better.'

'There is no need to take that tone with me.'

'Watch it baldy or you'll find yourself stuffed up the input. Then God himself knows what we'd see on the tape.'

8

There was so much convincing menace in it that the man recoiled a step with his feet in a tangle. Keeping well back from the counter, he threw the folder across and a newly printed ivorine disk.

'There's your admission serial. Take it to room thirty-one and register. You will have to hurry.'

'And where's thirty-one, then?'

'Across the hall. It has the number on the door.'

'A great piece of forward thinking. I'll look out for you for another friendly chat.'

Thirty-one was more a broad corridor than a room. One wall held a long computer bank with a feed slot at the near end for his admission disk. Once in the hole it trundled along a transparent track at a slow walking pace and he kept level, collecting batches of material at outfall points. Course notes, diagrams of the complex, tubes of micro tape, monthly issue of meal vouchers, house rules. Last in line, a neat oblong case to hold all his treasures, with a check list on the inside of the lid and his name freshly stencilled on the front.

He half expected a dummy hand to shove out for a shake, but there was only a plummy voice saying, 'Proceed to room thirty-seven for medi check.'

That was something now. Even mature students would not be expected to be carrying a laser in a shoulder clip.

There was nobody else in the room so he zipped smartly out of his jacket, wound the harness round the gun and fitted it in his document case.

Thirty-seven had a moving walkway that took off as soon as he stepped inside the door and carried him through five scanning alcoves. At the last station, he was revolved slowly, backed against a wall and a sharp thump in his left buttock told him that the Atlantic Federation had taken advantage of him again.

He was immune from all social diseases. But it was a dead liberty and the way things were going unnecessary at that.

9

He said, 'As God is my witness, I'll wreck the next machine that does that. Where have all the nurses gone with their soothing fingers and comely black tights?'

There was one with an auburn ringlet and a lapel sticker naming the name Christie Maclean looking startled as she peered out of a hatch. 'Mr Robert Cain?'

'The same.'

'What did you say?'

'Rhetoric. Simple rhetoric. Do you live in that hole?'

'Just a minute.'

She withdrew and he left his station and pushed his head and shoulders in the gap. It was a small monitoring room and she was gathering tape from every angle. A trim number, with a crotch length lab coat and a neat action.

'Well?'

'It's all right. You're category A-One-A. Physically able to sustain the course. I couldn't judge the mental side, naturally.'

'It needs investigating. I'll come and lie on your couch and you can try free association.'

'That's not very original Mr Cain. You'd be surprised how many people say that.'

'Nothing would surprise me.'

'Then you have a blunted sense of wonder. Turn left outside and you will see the way to your dormitory block.'

'And when do you come off duty? This curt professional mask can't be all there is of Christie Maclean.'

A pleasantly rounded index finger hovered over a push button. She said, 'When I press it, you have a couple of seconds to get your grinning head out of that hatch. If you delay we shall never know whether you could have finished the course or not.'

'You wouldn't do that.'

She pressed it and he was out with the closing edge riffling the hair on his scalp.

In the male living wing, he found his cell had all the equipment he would need for private study. There was a composite dressing chest and a work console that filled one wall, a narrow bed with a blue and white check coverlet and a translucent sliding hatch in the solar wall leading out to a small balcony.

Off left was a wash room with a shower cubicle, off right was a deep storage closet and his trunk was already there, leaning slightly off true on one dented end.

Cain took a shower, hitched a plain green towel round his waist, lit his pipe and roamed thoughtfully around his pad. He came to rest opposite the pile of data he had drawn from reception and leafed through the folder.

He was registered for a crash course on The Science of Mental Life. There were six avenues to explore. Statistics in Psychology. Mental Parameters. Current Research. History of Psychological Theories. Interpersonal Relationships, and one labelled Seminar. Well, it couldn't be bad to tank up on what made the whole world tick. He had done less agreeable things in the line of duty.

It should have been a good cover. Every fifth year any citizen of the Atlantic Federation had the right to take a six month break from his work to bone up on a topic of his choice, either with a view to changing his job or out of simple interest.

Maybe he was reading too much into the car incident. Either that or his cover had been blown for some time and there was a hangover from a previous operation with some disgruntled sod out to settle an old score.

That had to be it, because the current brief was vague enough.

In fact it was no brief at all. Just a directive to get himself on the campus and look around.

A shaft of late sunlight dropping on his balcony moved him to do that thing.

The window fittings had not been used for some time. The last resident must have liked his air washed and filtered by the plant. He had to take a shoe and beat at a release catch before he could get out.

He was overlooking a deep well with a small garden area. Small, foreshortened figures were taking an exercise walk round a fountain with a black basalt nymph tipping a steady stream out of a cornucopia. Two of the enclosing solar walls were dead plain. The one on the right and his own were studded with a regular pattern of balconies.

It was not much to jerk his mental life into a spasm and there was a nipping and eager air rising up his kilt. He turned back to his nest and was galvanized into a smart belated leap that brought him to the glass as the spring return shot the panel home a final centimetre and closed it with a muted click.

The seal was absolute, hardly showing a hair crack. There was no handle. It was ridiculous but it was a fact of life.

Cain leaned over his balcony and shouted 'Hi.'

Acoustic engineering was too good. His voice was lost. Nobody looked up. The nymph went on emptying her horn of plenty. He took off his towel and flapped it. A girl in a red tabard sitting on the edge of the fountain waved back and then went right on dabbling her fingers.

He reckoned he could be there all night with hoar frost gathering on his beard.

It was no way to begin a stint on the mental life. He leaned out to look at the balcony below. Staggered but overlapping. Hardly three metres off. Hanging at arms length he could get his feet on the rail and step in.

It was a shrewd estimate. When his feet grounded on the baluster, he still had a margin of stretch. But flattening his diaphragm was not good for his towel. He felt it slip away and move off in free fall.

Ducking under the canopy and jumping down, he was in time to see it fall in the fountain. The girl in red fished it out and leaned over to drape it on the centrepiece.

Then she waved again and pointed to it. It was okay, he hadn't lost it, he could pick it up at his leisure.

Cain moved to the solar window and pressed his nose to the glass to beat refraction. It was a room much like his own, but the bed coverlet was pink and white and there was a trail of discarded clothing leading from the outside door marking the owner's progress to the shower.

It was an interesting sequence. First a shoe, then a white coat, then another shoe, then a tricky equaliser with a repeating pattern of little sea horses and one leg of a pair of tights with the rest going out of the composition because of the angle.

He was focusing on that at the risk of dislocating his neck when the owner appeared at floor level bent on a collecting ploy, auburn ringlet in free fall.

Balling a fist, he hammered on the glass and she looked up, a puzzled stooper.

It was no sight to see at the end of a busy day, but medics learn to take the rough with the smooth.

He pointed up. Then at the lock, then at her door. It was a nice performance lost to the boards. She backed off still on hands and knees and there was a stage wait.

When she reappeared in a lime green housecoat carrying a heavy wrench and opened the hatch on a short chain, Cain said, 'Hurry it up. I'm on a cold floor.'

'That surely is not my fault. What are you doing on my balcony in a state of nature?'

'I could say that I was inflamed by your proud beauty, but it would be a politic lie. The truth is not so interesting.'

'Well, let's have it. I might just believe it. Truth I like.'

'I got locked out on my balcony. Just immediately above. I'll just nip along back there, if you'll open the door and step discreetly aside.'

'This is the resident female staff floor. It's not too easy.'

'Lend me your wrench. If asked I'll say I was fixing a faucet.'

Dark brown eyes with very white cornea considered him for a short count. Then she unhooked the chain and let him in.

'Hold it a minute. I've got a trench coat that might fit.'

She went over to the closet and rummaged around, coming up with a heavy khaki job, complete with epaulettes and stud fasteners.

When he had it on, he felt that much ahead. 'What's this then? What's a svelte, ginger medic doing with a man's top coat in her locker?'

'Questions, questions. Just be grateful. It belongs to a friend. Drop it down on the balcony. But wedge your door or you could be off on another cycle and I wouldn't be so generous and accommodating again.'

'Well, thank you. Thank you. I'll remember you. Should you have a problem and need the services of a sympathetic friend, knock twice on your ceiling and I'll be with you in a trice.'

'Even a trice would be an improvement on what you were in this trip.'

'If you have a fault, Ginger, and I freely admit a man would have to look close to find one, it is this ready wit. This is the second time you've had the good hand. Look out for the swing of fortune's wheel. I'll be seeing more of you. Or, at least, to keep in line with your passion for truth. I'll be seeing you.'

There was no traffic on the floor until he reached the elevator trunk. As he waited for service, a cage halted at the stop and a half dozen homing resident female staff flocked out in a conversational twitter.

There was a lull at his beard and a pop-eyed girl in a blue tabard gave a small 'Eek' as she noticed his bare feet.

Six pairs of eyes gave him a close scan and a babble broke out as he stepped into his cage and was lifted away. It would make a talking point at that. If anybody had been strangled in her tub, he was suspect number one.

Back in his pad, Cain dressed, weighed his laser in his hand and debated where to put it. Finally he fixed the harness and shoved it in its clip. Later, he could get his room organized. As of now, he needed a meal and a drink and a little quiet reflection.

Before going out, he took the coat, intending to drop it on the balcony below. Without thinking, he checked through the pockets. No dice. Not even a collection of fluff. No markings either. No name tab, no manufacturer's label. A very non-committal artifact. Too impersonal by a good sea league.

He went systematically over the seams. Then the fastenings, giving each one a twist. When he had it, he considered it with simple disbelief. What was the point of it?

The micro transmitter was a hexagon on a two milli-metre diameter that fitted in the hollow of a perforated press stud.

He screwed the stud back in place and went thought-fully to the balcony, shoving a chair against the trick door. Leaning out, he dropped the coat to the balcony below. Taking careful aim he pitched the bijou trans-mitter into the fountain. Anybody listening in from now on would get a low gurgle.

The corridor was filling up. New entrants fresh from a fact-finding tour were dodging about. Friendly, but guarded. At this stage nobody wanted to get stuck with an alliance they might live to regret.

His room number was F29. On the left, in 28, he had a dapper character, with a dark narrow face who was clipping his name slip in the slot on his hatch. Clearly one who liked to know who he was at all times.

Cain stopped and read it off. 'Trevor Sturgess. How does it go, Bud? Cain. Robert Cain. Your nearest neighbour up the alley.'

Sturgess completed his chore, patted out a wrinkle and stood back to admire the effect. 'They ought to make these tabs a millimetre smaller all round, then they'd go in without any trouble.'

'Or increase the size of the slot.'

'Could be. Cain, you say? That's a familiar name. I've heard it before some place. Would you be from Chester City?'

'Not from Chester City.'

'Then I guess not. What course?'

'Mental Life. Probing that heap where every man is a stranger to himself.'

Sturgess allowed himself a tight smile of satisfaction. 'Then I shan't see much of you. I'm on Technology of Visual Aids.' He moved inside and closed his door.

Farther up a tall negro in a grey suit was using a key on 30. Cain said 'Hi', and got a nod and a signal from a large spatulate thumb.

He went on to the well head and studied a diagram of the complex. The students' diner was in the basement of the block he was in. Over the way were lecture theatres, libraries, research areas, all the paraphernalia of the learning process. Admin was located over the reception hall. Recreation was mainly centred in the fourth block that closed the square. It was a neat space saving design, easy to control, with facilities for four thousand. Still, over any five-year period it could handle forty thousand which was a fair enough proportion for the professional level in one city.

The diner itself was self service with long banks of dispensers filling three walls. He fed a ticket in a slot and four disks rattled down a chute. Choice of four items. Soup. Main Course. Pud. Coffee. Or he could go mad and have four Picton Specials which, if the pictograph told no lie, was chicken and rice with ground nut sauce.

Over a six month stint it was going to be a rough assignment and he felt a stirring of self pity. Somebody in the department would be having a deep belly laugh. He settled for the Special with a slab of lemon meringue pie and two cups of black coffee.

The hall stretched away like an exercise in perspective. With four thousand at the trough, it was plain and functional with tables clewed firmly to the deck and disposal bollards set between every four tables.

Along one wall, above the dispensers was a narrow metal catwalk for a patrolling warder to see fair play and stop any move of disorientated diners to drop smaller students into the grinders.

It was only a quarter full and acoustic engineering was so good that it might have been empty.

He joined a couple at a table for six and they stopped an animated chat and stared at him over their Picton Specials. The girl was a severe blonde with a blue bandeau and a feline mouth. The man was heavily handsome with a blue chin and tufts of black hair on the backs of his fingers.

Cain said, 'Carry on. Don't let me disturb your nosh. Feel free to indulge in any practice however intimate. Animal hunger has driven me to this place and I shall soon be gone.'

The girl said frostily, 'I beg your pardon. What did you say?'

'Just a civility.'

'Oh.'

They exchanged one of the nine significant levels of eyebrow raising and conversation died the death.

As the evening wore on, Cain found himself questioning the motive of his department. He reckoned he could have been at any one of a thousand provincial polytechs. There was nothing sinister on the set, unless it was a conspiracy against the Life Force itself.

His brief had been minimal and cryptic. There had not even been personal contact with his chief in Department K. Just a directive on the answering service when he called in for weekly report. But all the paper work had been done, unseen strings had been pulled. He was in with official status as a student without the usual preliminaries.

Maybe they were putting him away for a rest period. The last affair had not gone too well. Luck had got him out of it alive with Grant and Ferriby dead, but a whole circuit of Southern Hem agents had been hammered out of shape. It would be years before they rebuilt the links.

Still it was a game where there was no final prize and no let up. Yesterday was always long dead. Memories were short.

He looked round the bar which was only partly full and carried his drink to a free-standing display panel used to advertise free time activities on the campus. Political groups. Athletic leagues. Weekend schemes of pleasure which included a Fell Walking Club—already well subscribed with a couple of dozen names scrawled on the *sign here* slip. All highly regular and commendable.

He tracked back to the political wing. There was a group calling themselves *The Vorticists*, with a meeting for twenty-one hundred. The convener was one Adrian Stringer and the name seemed familiar.

He moved to the Fell Walking notice again and there sure enough was A. Stringer at the head of the list as the party leader. A man of the mountains, a prophet even.

Cain looked at his strap watch, twenty-forty-five on the nose. Time to take in the Vorticist inaugural meeting and show interest in his fellow man. Though what new political angle could appear in this sophisticated day was a black mystery.

It was not much clearer an hour later, sitting with a mixed bag of thirty or so of the inmates in one of the well-equipped conference rooms on the top floor of the recreation block.

Maybe the rarified air was starving his brain, but he could not see what the organizers were getting at.

Stringer was a round man. Wiry hair in an upstanding dark brown fuzz, sheared by a topiarist into a rough sphere. Round eyes, with small mad pupils. Small round mouth, moistened from time to time by a busy tongue. Plump, with chubby hands and small feet in white sneakers. Not a natural fell walker at that.

The party label was coined from its founder one Marshall Vort, a professor in Dianetics. The sayings of Marshall Vort cropped up every so often in the text.

On the whole, he seemed to be pitching for the right of the individual to be an anarchist. Man was born to be free, but found himself in the closest straight jacket that history had ever devised. In the past, there had been loopholes for the human spirit to peer through, but from the beginning of the second millenium the growing efficiency of the state machine had nailed it good. Now a man was under surveillance from the cradle to the grave, fed, clothed, educated and deprived of the right to suffer. All wrong. It stunted his psychical growth. Feel free to do whatever you want to do was Vort's advice.

Another strand which did not seem to lie too neatly with the main argument was the idea of an elite corps at the top of the human heap. On the other hand, it was good flattering psychology to feed the faithful that they were a master group who would be in charge of the new deal. What happened to a party member who might have anarchical ideas about that was not defined.

The meeting closed with a date given for another session at the same time, same night, the following week. On the way out, Cain helped himself to a selection of hand out material. Before he raised his voice in debate, he reckoned he should take a look at the facts.

It was still early, but it had been a busy day. He stopped off at a bar on the third level which was tricked out with black polystyrene beams and copper warming pans. Not much business was being done and the sturdy girl at the dispenser, dressed for the decor in an open-laced black bodice with a dirndl skirt, had one shoe off and was massaging her left instep with her right hand as she leaned back against the reredos.

The action was testing her laces to near destruction and Cain reckoned that a good Vorticist would lean over the counter with a snipper, but he beat down his Id and fell back on urbanity, 'A nice place you have here.'

'It's all right.'

'Not too busy. When does the riot start?'

She put on her shoe with a small hesitation as though she had debated whether or not to bury the heel in his head. 'Look. Do you want a drink? Just name it and I'll get it.'

'That's fair enough. Calvados. The big measure. Have one yourself. Bring a little sparkle to that disillusioned eye.'

'All right. But don't think it buys you any favours.'

'Such a thought had never entered my head.'

'Then your head is a very non representative item. You'd be surprised at the trouble I have. The intellectual life seems to inflame the student body.'

'Your jolly rustic costume will play its part in that.'

She sipped her brandy with a delicate shudder and looked at him reflectively. 'What are you doing in this depressed corner of hell?'

'Just following my interest on a short course.'

The warming liquor brought a mood of confidence. She leaned rounded elbows on the bar. 'So am I.'

'What are you doing there, then?'

'Part time. My lousy department wouldn't wear a full grant. So I'm working my passage.'

'In the highest tradition of the self made woman. Here's to success and confusion to the tight wads. Have another.'

'Thank you. No. There's work to do. I have some notes to play back and I wouldn't want them all confused in my head.'

'Well. I'll see you around the halls and covered ways. Don't burn your candle out. Cain, Robert Cain, should you want to borrow a pencil.'

'Brigitta Ross. I'll remember. Keep it sharpened just in case. But as I said there are a lot on offer.'

Cain found his corridor as quiet as on arrival. He went out on his balcony and leaned over. Either Christie Maclean had gone early to bed or was still out and about.

He heaved his battered trunk onto his bed and methodically unpacked into the dressing chest.

When it was empty he stood it on end on the floor and checked the frame. Reinforced structural members on the hinge side were undamaged which said a lot for the technicians who had devised it.

Before going any farther he took his shaver out of its case and walked around the room with it flat on his palm. Its selector disk remained rock steady. Unless there was something very special, there was no electronic pick up in the area. He tried the washroom, the closet and even the balcony. Clean as a hound's tooth.

Working on the trunk again, he shifted a small ferrule on the short edge of the lid and pulled up a long telescopic antenna. Beside it, another narrow slot held a fine multicore wandering lead and he plugged the free end into the base of the shaver. Turning the selector to a new setting, he said, 'K5. Mission twelve. Report one.'

There was a two second wait and a clipped female voice said 'Identify.'

'Rue.'

'Go ahead K5.'

'On site. Incident on arrival. Possibly an accident, but could be an attempt to hold off an enquiry. Should be noted in case there is a second.'

'Will do.'

'I want all the information there is about the Vorticist movement. Where can I pick it up?'

'No arrangements have been made yet for contact.

21

Meanwhile follow the amber sequence. Expect to hear tomorrow in the afternoon.'

'Nothing for me? Like why I'm here?'

'No. Over and out.'

Stretched on his narrow bed, he could have been at the heart of a pyramid. There was no sound from left or right, below or above. Whatever else, Picton Polytech had to offer, it was quiet. It was some time since he had been so thrown in on himself.

A mental cog slipped the escapement and he was back in time to another dark corner with Joe Grant saying quietly in his ear, 'It's not natural. Nothing should be as still as this.' Then it had all happened at once, house lights, cross fire, Joe going for the door in a heroic sprint. Himself nicked by a ricochet and streaming with warm blood waiting for the pay off.

His fingers found the scar. A cracked pitcher goes oftenest to the well. He was cracked all right to be still at his trade. Maybe the mental life bit was overdue. He could end up with his occupation gone.

CHAPTER TWO

Cain squared up to the only clear panel of wall he could find, which was a metre strip beside the door. Palms flat, fingers up, shoulder height, left foot advanced half a pace, he took a deep slow breath, held it and began to push for a count of six.

Light from the solar wall had wakened him early and after fighting a rearguard for twenty minutes, he had rolled out of the sack and started in on his daily session of isometric drills.

Isometrics suited him. They took little time, needed no equipment and were less self advertising than a stint in the gym.

Remembering the text, he was concentrating on his shoulders, back and upper arms, having worked through a routine for his neck which should assure that his head stayed upright on its stalk for the next twenty-four hours.

At the count of five, he was developing a lot of power with his mind focused on the chore. When the double panel shifted from its site and shot out into the corridor releasing a tidal flow of pea-sized white granules from the cavity wall, he was an astonished man and was half way through the hole before he could throw out an anchor.

His surprise was matched by the janitor of floor F, who was walking down the centre of the aisle with a brisk military step and got his feet in a tangle coming to an emergency stop.

Bent double like an ergo gnome after impact, with his

peaked cap slewed off line, his face was on the same level as Cain's and he put the establishment angle in a choky sibilant voice. 'You shouldn't of done that Mr Cain. That's pure 'ooliganism that is. If I'd been one step farther on my illegitimate business, it might've been very nasty. Very nasty. What was you doing in there if I might be so bold as to ask the question?'

'Just a few setting up exercises.'

'Setting down, more like. If every student on my floor was to go doing that where would we be then? It'd be like the Last Days of Popeye come again.'

Cain pulled himself out of his hole, stepping in a crunchy mound and brushing himself off.

Through the gap, the janitor was doing the same, straightening his cap and pulling a note book from the top pocket of his coveralls.

The name tab on the same pocket said, Abe Gargan. He had a long sad face and had lost one of his upper front teeth in the rearguard fight against encroaching time.

Cain said, 'You have the right of it, Abe. Now we know why this place is silent as any tomb. It's all this insulation. Now just hand up the panel and we'll push it back. Then a brisk bash with the cleaner's besom and nobody will know the difference.'

'*I'll* know the difference Mr Cain. And there's no call for vulgarity. It'll have to be done proper. Cost about twenty credits that. Man's time and materials. Just sign 'ere and I'll 'ave it done.'

'Okay. Do that thing. Send me the bill. I wouldn't want the polytech to founder on my account.'

'You'll get the bill right enough. Just take more care, Mr Cain. Three damage reports and you could be asked to leave in ignominity.'

'That's not nice. I'll stick to an outside wall.'

A brief smile lightened Gargan's melancholy face. 'That's right. Then if you go through, all the mess will be on the grass and that's a job for the outside staff.'

Cain worked through the rest of the sequence, took a shower, read the lecture schedule and loaded himself with the sets of notes he might need.

Breakfast was a brutalized stampede around the dispensers with two janitors on the catwalk to see fair play. He came out of the ruck with two bowls of porridge, a devilled egg, and a beaker of hot chocolate, having to the best of his knowledge and belief shoved his disks into the slots for kidney and bacon with coffee and toast on the side.

There were some sly movers about and he reckoned it was time the janitors were armed to pick off the ringleaders.

Through the press, he saw his negro neighbour in a blue denim jacket with a stand up collar balancing a tray on one massive hand and looking around for an empty seat. He beat a way toward him and they made out to a table in the centre aisle.

When they were settled, the man said, 'I've seen you before some place.'

'F29. The next pad.'

'That's it. That's so. Saw you come in. You've got a right creep on the other side.'

'Sturgess.'

'Could be. A bloodless little nit. That's a rough meal you have there. Do you have some kind of problem?'

'I don't understand it too well. It's not what I thought.'

'That figures. You have to be real vigilant here to stay alive. What's in the pot?'

'Chocolate.'

'It looks real nasty. Here pour some down the hole and top it up with this.' He reached round into a hip pocket and brought out a flat gun metal flask with a screw top.

Cain recognized that he had come ill-prepared to the academic life and took it with gratitude. He said, 'That's a very civil offer. Cain's the name. Robert Cain.'

'Arthur Delacroix. Call me Art.'

Delacroix took back his flask and used it generously to lace his coffee. Cain tried one of his porridge bowls, pushed it away and worked cautiously on his egg.

A small explosion of force caused him to lift his head. Art had nailed a young man's sleeve to the table top with his fork.

'What do you want, Boy?'

'Just the salt. I was just stretching over for the salt.'

'Were you brought up in some barn? You could ask for it. Sure you weren't going for my bread roll?'

'Sure I'm sure. Are you crazy or something?'

'Okay just move real slow and take it.'

Cain said pacifically, 'What's your angle then? What are you doing on this dog's island?'

'Just a pause for reflection. I got this feeling I was in like a shallow grave. So having the five-year option, I took this course on cybernetics.'

'What were you doing before?'

'Actualizer Distribution Inc. Installation and that. Meeting the public in its own pad. Very rough. Nothing so queer as folk in their own home with the snick on the latch. You'd be surprised where people want an actualizer fixed. What's your angle?'

'Actualizers again. At the other end of the link. Science correspondent.'

'Now it's surprising I didn't recognize you. I'd guess I've seen every programme on the frame at one time or another.'

'Back room stuff. Just supplying a few facts for the myth makers to pull about.'

'No credits even?'

'Just that inner glow that comes from a job well done.'

Delacroix swung his left arm in a wide gesture to look at his strap watch, a massive navigator's job designed for a sidereal fix. His neighbour made anxious by his cuff choked nervously on his toast.

'I'll have to leave you Cain. See you again. Time for a practical on the android cortex. Sober stuff. Watch their eyes and don't give anything away.'

'That's a very fine time disk.'

'A gift from a satisfied client. Wanted her actualizer in the shower as I recall. You missed a lot in your ivory tower.'

Cain watched him make a loose limbed progress through the diner, finished his Gaelic Chocolate and followed after.

His own lecture room was on the same floor as the Cybernetics outfit in a complex labelled Department of Experimental Psychology. Twenty students shuffled in and settled at individual consoles. A fair girl in a grey caftan put her head on her pad and went quietly to sleep as though she had missed a lot.

Two minutes before time, a disembodied circular head appeared at the glass port in the hatch and Adrian Stringer hurried into the room and settled himself at the master desk. He ignored his students and busied himself with the programme selector. Smack on the stroke of nine he lifted his head and said 'Stand by.' Then he shoved over a lever and the empty space on his right filled with a standing figure.

It was the head of the department, Professor George Cleator, an angular egghead in a tweed jacket and a bow tie and they were off on a closed circuit actualizer hook up for the inaugural lecture on Memory with a quotation from Proust about the stimulating qualities of a morsel of cake steeped in a teaspoonful of tea.

Stringer would have done well to walk around feeding that seminal potion to his flock. Two joined the girl in exhausted slumber. Others looked out of the window at the city and a distant shimmer of the river.

That view was cut off as Stringer darkened the room and began to synchronize illustrative material with the flowing word. The onset of a new night stirred the girl out

27

of hibernation and she sat up with a delicate yawn and fluffed the hair from her neck.

Seeing Cleator fresh from sleep was a rugged option and her mouth stayed open while she sorted it all out.

The text was no help. He was saying that it was not a thing like a cold sausage on a fork, but more a flame burning from an unseen jet. Dynamic. Plasma held in a force field, if they liked to see it that way. A holographic structure.

Conviction grew on her that it was a false dawn. She looked around in open eyed wonder, then settled again for another refreshing sleep.

One advantage of the system was that Cleator was not distracted and went right on. To his own satisfaction, he listed three types of memory. The simple reflex that made a bare foot choose another place for a landfall after it had stepped on a tack. More complex middle length persistence lasting for days or weeks and the long term with recall triggered by association.

He went on for thirty minutes before Stringer pulled the plug and the image faded unevenly. A fault in the circuitry which would have had Delacroix reaching for his trouble shooting kit left Cleator's snapping white teeth as the last part of the mirage to fold. It would have settled the fair girl's hash if she had been awake to see.

As it was it left a sinister after taste.

Stringer cleared his throat. 'That's all there is. You have the transcripts and the work tape. I suggest you run through once today while it's all fresh and bubbling in your mind. That way you keep ahead. Don't think you can stock pile a week's take and do it all at a go. Completed work rolls can be dropped in any tutoring computer in the department and your score will be recorded on your log sheet. Anything over the fifty percentile keeps your nose clean. Three below forty and you'll get a ticket. Knock it off now for a fifteen minute spell.'

Cain had two more classes, the last timed for 1400. At 1445 he was bemused, but free as a bird. He went out of the main door into mild sunlight.

There was a lot of sky about and white clouds moving inland from the sea. It was like coming out of a dark tunnel.

Up ahead there was a trim figure in a brief tartan kilt mainly red and dark green, which had a pleasing rhythmic swing and he hurried to catch up.

It was the Maclean and he said, 'Where are we going then in our tribal finery?'

'Oh, it's you. The intrepid bird man.'

As a psychologist he could analyze that in a flash. 'What kind of an answer is that? What have you to hide? You are repressing the truth, because it conflicts with your self-regarding instinct. Have no fear. However sordid your mission you can confide in me. Think of me as your doctor, a compassionate and discreet figure. You can tell me anything.'

'Dear God. Why did I come out of the front door? There's a staff entrance. I could have used that. But no, I have to switch just once.'

'There's a pattern in it somewhere. Lie down and close your eyes and we'll dig around for it.'

'Look, if you must know, I'm going down to a store to buy a new toothbrush.'

'Good, good. That's better. Now you're facing your problem. Frank confession of motive. But why the kilt?'

'Public decency regs.'

'That figures. All right, Mac, we'll let it go at that.'

'Thank you very much.'

'You got the mac back, Mac?'

'Yes, I got it.'

'Very nice of you to lend it. What would your friend have to say if he knew you'd been using his gear to succour a passing nude?'

'Not much. I haven't seen him for some time actually.'

'Jilted you then? Found another hook for his topcoat?'

'You ask too many questions. In fact you talk too much altogether. Which way are you going?'

'I'll walk beside you to the toothbrush store. I have some small items to buy.'

'I'd get a dog and then you could talk to it and it'd look up at you with big sad eyes.'

'And what does your friend do to keep his niche in the social pyramid?'

'He's a Civil Engineer. Attached to City Hall. Name of Donovan, Cyril Donovan. To forestall the next question.'

'Civil Cyril.'

'I am a fool to speak. I might have known your child mind would make that hook up.'

'Is he a short, stocky man with an upstanding quiff?'

'If he was a short stocky man that coat you borrowed would flap round his ankles.'

'Do you know any short stocky men with upstanding quiffs?'

Christie Maclean stopped dead and faced him, 'What are you on about now? Go away. Go and pester somebody else or I'll call a guard.'

Having chosen to walk they were following the static way, a narrow footpath clewed to the first floor of major tower blocks with open flyovers at the intersections. She had stopped midway along a suspended section, two metres wide with hand rails either side. Eight metres below, the moving walkway was empty. There was a lull in movement about the city.

The sudden stop brought confusion to a man who had followed them out on to the open sector. He was ten metres from his corner and could not go back.

He came right on and Christie Maclean looked at him with a startled eye. Short and stocky with black hair standing like a cock's comb, he had a hard pale face that looked out of place in the light of day.

Cain had backed to the far rail so that the man had to

pass between them. When he was level he looked left and right without change of expression.

Cain moved with deceptive speed and she was looking at his back and the newcomer had disappeared against the rail.

Still asking questions, but with a nasty bite, Cain was saying, 'What do you want then?'

There was no reply, but a flurry of activity. Cain sidestepped to dodge a knee aimed for his crotch, took the lower leg in a double grip and heaved away. Placed as he was with the rail in the small of his back, the man was set up to illustrate simple mechanical law. He pivoted through a hundred and eighty degrees of arc, appeared briefly against the railings, head down and slid away in free fall for the distant walkway.

Cain said, 'He shouldn't have done that. He might have done me a serious injury.'

Medical training to the fore, the girl was leaning over her side of the flyover watching the body shift slowly away on the moving pedestrian way. Nobody had noticed. She turned around eyes blazing. 'You killed him. You killed that man.'

'Listen.'

'Not any more. I'll have Public Safety pick you up.'

She was off at a sprint, ringlet bobbing emotionally left and right. It was a nice leg action, very feminine and Cain would have liked to watch it all along the course, but she had to be stopped.

It took twenty metres and she struggled like a cat when he caught up. He said, 'Listen,' again and, all movement damped down, she tried to bite his neck.

Cain had a small debate with himself, clear thinking was not helped by a warm ambience of sandalwood and distracting pneumatic pressures, but he came down on the lesser of two evils. 'Listen, you crazy nut. Hold still and I'll show you something.'

'An exhibitionist as well as a murderer. No thank you.'

31

Cain transferred his grip, got a hand free, fished inside his pocket and shoved an oblong plaque in front of her nose. It had an official look and she studied it reluctantly.

'What is it?'

'You must be pig ignorant. Have you never seen a Federal seal?'

'So you have a licence to kill people?'

Cautiously he let her go. 'Now just walk along and relax. First thing, keep this information to yourself. No running along to Cyril for instance.'

'Go on.'

'I have a connection with the Federal Public Safety Office.'

'What are you doing in Picton?'

'Even Public Safety details have the five-year option. I'm following a regular course. Certain parties may not believe that. In fact there was an attempt to drop a hire car on my head when I came in to the terminal. Now all I want is the quiet life. But not carried to the ultimate in a casket.'

She stopped again and considered him. The exercise had given her a good colour and small freckles around her nose were plain to see. Eyes were very dark brown, almost luminous. Her own private debate took longer, but finally she said reluctantly, 'All right. I'll go along with that. But no more surprises. Your credibility is wearing thin.'

They reached a junction with static ways going off in a fan and a stair head for the lower deck.

Christie Maclean said, 'This is where I go down.'

'I'm going across to the next block. I'll be seeing you then.'

'Give ample warning. I'll have to think about that.'

A keening wail from afar underlined the point. An ambulance was on its way to pick up a client.

Cain spent a little time at the information board in the shopping precinct. There was a post office with a *poste restante* service in the basement of the tower core. The amber routine was only minimum cover. Nobody was going to get excited about a collection of political handouts.

At the same time, experience was making him cautious and he circled through a couple of department stores before he went down on the escalator.

'Is there a package for Anderson?'

'Mr M. J. Anderson?'

'The same.'

'Identity serial please.'

He had it ready and shoved it under the grille with a frank, open smile.

'Yes, there's a package. Sign the receipt.'

When he had it, he circled again through the precinct, bought himself a flask and had it filled with rye, a potent fragment to shore against the ruins of time.

He stopped at a garden department mainly devoted to window boxes, jardinieres and hanging baskets. There was a half metre diameter sphere on a bronze chain bursting out all over with vermilion geraniums.

He said, 'I'd like that sent up to the Polytech. Cain F29. Can do?'

The wizened oldster in Lincoln Green who was i/c the sector, said, 'Surely, son. We'll send it along. Here's the chit. Pay at the desk and as soon as the credit's cleared, it'll be on its way. You did well there. There'll be colour in your home for many a month to come. But watch where you set it up. There's a fair weight in that. Wouldn't do to pull a piece out of your roof and have it fall on your head when you was hard at it.'

'You're right. There are distractions enough. I'll fix it good. Give me a couple of metres of chain and a shackle.'

He threaded the complex again, coming out at the town's main library, showed his student's pass and got a punched strip giving him sixty minutes in a research cubicle linking him as though by an umbilical cord to the whole reservoir of human knowledge to date.

Enclosed in the acoustic shell of the booth, he felt all the pressure of it. There was just too much on tap. So much that it had become a burden. Maybe the mechanical extension of memory was a bad thing. A man was only geared to cope with his own biological limit and not all of that. The collection of information had not produced wisdom.

The video on the console glowed with a girl's face featuring large round horn rimmed glasses in the best librarian tradition and a brisk voice asked, 'What service can I give you?'

'Nothing, love, at the distance. Just stay wholly vigilant and I'll call as and when.'

She gave a tight smile and withdrew. He tipped his package on the desk and began to sort through it.

The department had done well in the time. There was a profile on Marshall Vort, an account of the Vorticist movement, a list of known local groups and a selection of Vorticist literature, some of which duplicated what he already had.

He took Vort first.

Born in 2083 the *guru* was now sixty-four. But from his most recent picture looked a lot younger. Whatever he was doing was doing him nothing but good.

He had been an academic of wide interests, having shifted about on the teaching side from Cybernetics and Psychology, over to a short stint in Political Economy and finally coming to rest as a specialist in Dianetics, the science of mind power and mental health.

There was a book by him on the topic titled *Hello Wall* and the professed aim of the work was to guide communication between the individual and his fellow man and the environment. There were training routines to follow, mental exercises and graded tasks to judge progress.

Eventually the pilgrim would win out to a true under-standing of his own identity with the suggestion that this would put him ahead in some major way.

Cain reckoned it was dubious. It was a fifty-fifty chance that given complete self-knowledge a man would hate what he saw and want to die.

The department had made a brief critical survey of the system and judged it to be an ill-considered hodge-podge of jargon-riddled, schoolboy psychology stiffened with a few technical gimmicks from the experimental psychology lab.

Vort was claiming a break through into a new religion which would replace all the outdated beliefs in the world and equip the new man with the right psychic tool to deflower the future.

In fact, claimed the department's reader, he had come up with a stone age adze with a plastic handle. Which was not to say, however, that nobody had been taken in. There was a large membership, sending subscriptions to Vort to finance his contemplation.

The easy mechanistic mumbo-jumbo had a big appeal to the lazy minded young, who lacked the energy and the ability to think the thing through on their own account. They were glad of a leader who could absolve them from all personal responsibility and give them a formula to follow however banal. It was, when all was said, no more stupid than many another religious system which had been swallowed whole by untold millions.

Cain turned to the Vorticist movement. This had grown first as a by product of the philosophizing bit. Its aims were to produce the political background in which the religious shrub could come to full blossom.

But it had outgrown its first purpose or the two elements had been fused into a single strand. The Vorticist Programme had the same clear objectives as any other political group—to get power for itself, to keep that power, and to deny power to anybody else. Its significant shortfall was a lack of any coherent social programme.

Other than a non-specific claim that all would be free to do their thing and reach a new and fuller maturity, it wisely preferred to keep the detail out of open scrutiny.

There were cells in all the higher education centres, openly registered. The establishment seemingly was not over worried. So far there had been no concerted push to get representatives on Regional Councils or on the Federal Senate.

Vort's last public appointment had been at Picton Polytech, a relatively minor post for a man with global ambition. Now he had dropped from the teaching scene and was directing operations from a private research centre which he had set up on a one time holiday camp site near Grasmere.

Maybe he knew Adrian Stringer personally. That intrepid Fell Walker could be keeping in touch on his weekly trips. For that matter other Lakeland enthusiasts might be doing the same. Every crag was abristle with fugitives from the termite city at the weekend.

Cain shredded the data and dropped it down the paper waste disposer. He probably had as much information in his head about the Vorticist Movement as the average member. It didn't add up to a great deal. For his money it was just another body dedicated to pushing the frontier of irrelevance farther back. Why the department had gone to the length of planting him at Picton was a black mystery. But one that he should be told about. He could imagine Angus Fraser, dour and unsmiling, making the switch. 'Send Cain. Do him good. Educate the ignorant bastard. Don't tell him why, just let him sweat a little. Don't pass any expense vouchers, he won't have any legitimate expenses in a place like that.'

Cain left the library and took a walkway to the waterfront. A hundred metre wide strip of tree-lined boulevard ran for a kilometre either way from the centre square where there had once been terminal buildings for cross river ferries.

There was also a top deck cantilevered on a single row of slender columns. A nice piece of town planning though at close quarters every plane surface was closely inscribed with *graffiti*. The planners were ahead of the planned for.

He climbed a narrow companion, walked along for a spell and then leaned on the baluster watching the people and looking out across the river.

There was still a good deal of warmth in the sun and there was an agreeable marine smell. A tall girl walked by, dark hair in a shoulder length elastic bell, short magenta tabard, long, smooth athletic legs. A credit to evolution.

Across the river, the twin city of the estuary was caught in gold cross light, a place of fable. But if he crossed the bridge to it, he knew it would be no different. There would be a baluster like the one he was leaning on, scrawls on every wall and an impersonal dark girl walking below caught in her own cage of consciousness.

There was a moral in it somewhere, but he couldn't identify it. Unless it was the old saw that the grass in the next valley was always greener.

He gave it up, followed the embankment up river for ten minutes then dropped to the bottom level at a walkway terminal and stepped on an express lane for the nearest point to the Polytech complex.

Business was brisker. As if on a signal, people had spilled out from the high density living units. Being his afternoon for significant thinking, he saw it as an illustration of the change of use of the few square kilometres of land where the city stood.

Up to three millenia back there had been no change for untold centuries. A man sitting on a tree stump could have looked around and seen the same basic family group grubbing about for something to throw in the pot. Then Bingo. In the flash of an iris eye shutter on the cosmic

37

time scale, he was surrounded by a million strangers and a concrete fantasia.

It was a lot to digest. No wonder the rehabilitation clinics were full to the sill. There had been too little time for the man to evolve and keep pace. The corporate mind had gone ahead of the individual mind. He could only make his mark on the nearest wall 'Fred was here'.

Abe Gargan whipped out of his lodge on the main landing for floor F. 'Just a minute, Mr Cain. What was you intending to do with this pergalorum, if I might be so bold?'

He pointed through his open door to a slatted crate with the hanging basket caged like a red beast. 'There's nowhere to 'ang it in your room, and that's a fact. You'll bring the place down round our ears.'

'That's all right. I have a piece of research in mind. Just put it on your trolley and wheel it along.'

'There's another thing. I've had the works department look at your wall. They don't like it.'

'That makes it unanimous. I don't like it. You don't like it. They don't like it.'

'It's no joke, Mr Cain. They 'ad to take out a whole section to get the insulation back. It's going to cost you plenty.'

'Don't worry Abe. I've got a rich uncle. They finished it then?'

'Not a 'alf hour back and the buildin' super inspected it. A new man. Very keen. Couldn't believe 'ow you'd done it. That is if you done it like you said.'

'Remarks like that knock at the roots of interpersonal relationships. Let's have the plant along.'

When he had it in his room he could see Abe's point. It looked a lot bigger than he expected. Wedging the balcony door he carried the crate through, used his laser to cut a couple of key bars and eased the basket out.

The chain was coiled below and he snapped its shackle

38

to his baluster where it overhung the balcony below, fixed the free hook to the basket and lowered away.

It was spot on. Nicely placed in the centre of her window. His hidden Adam, up for a breather, he also filled a tooth glass from his wash room and gave the plant a sundowner to show it was among friends.

Then he turned his attention to the new wall area. Gargan was right. From the door to the corner, right across his bed head, there was a change in colour. A whole fresh metre-deep panel had been put in.

He took his shaver and began a systematic check, working a centimetre a time from the door.

It took time and when he had it, he could hardly believe the kick of the dial and came at it again from another angle.

It was over the bed, less than half a metre from his sleeping ear. Did they expect him to be talking in his sleep then?

He took his laser, opened a cavity in the butt, and tipped the contents on his palm. Then he assembled a micro vibrator with a half centimeter cutting blade.

He made a small circular trepan and collected a handful of insulating pellets before the flow stopped.

When he had the device out on his pillow he was a surprised man. As far as he could see it was a one-way job. But not outgoing. Strictly for input. Somebody had it in mind to make a few sub liminal suggestions.

They would want to monitor the programme, so there was likely to be a pick up somewhere else. He was twenty minutes finding it. High up in the top left hand corner, a small hexagon sited in a large insulation pellet. They were getting to be like the sands of the desert.

He spent a little time sitting at his desk considering the angles. Obviously they should be left operational or other methods would be used which he might not identify. There was not much going on in his pad that need be kept from a public address system, but it might not always be so.

He took the transmitter in its pellet and strapped it to the underside of his bed with a strip of cellulose tape. The mini speaker went back in its hole and he put a small transmitter of his own beside it, set on the department's frequency. Whatever was said could be monitored. They could also send a stimulus signal to waken him so that he could hear the record while he was all systems go.

There was still the wall. His surgery had been delicate, but a close look would show the hair cracks. He made a quick trip to the basement book stall and rooted about for half a dozen pulp mags devoted to visual lechery.

The girl at the counter said 'Did you have a deprived childhood or something?'

'It's a research programme.'

'A *nasty* research programme, I'd say.'

'You weren't asked. Just ring up the score or I'll be over there for a little field work in sadism.'

He had enough to cover the whole wall. A bonus for Abe Gargan and his cleaning staff. Over the speaker site, he had a double page feature spread, a silicone injection job named Wanda, very acrobatic.

It was gruelling work and a distraction for a serious student. When it was done, he took a pull at his new hip flask to steady his nerve and rolled out his trunk. He carried it into the wash room and turned on the shower. Then he spoke softly into his own transmitter.

'K5.'

'Come in.'

'I want K1.'

'Hold.'

There was a ten second wait and a new voice grated impatiently in his ear. Angus Frazer said, 'What is it now? Aren't you happy on your vacation?'

'I'm getting very nervous. I want to know what in God's name I'm supposed to be doing in this penitentiary. I also want continuous monitoring on an RV50 I've set up.'

40

Early back to his pad, after a well fought meal in the diner and a brief visit to Brigitta Ross's bar, Cain settled for a work spell at his console. If there was any capital to be made out of the mission, it lay in getting a neck lock on the mental life bit. Who knew when a slice of arcane information might not come in handy?

He clipped in a tape on the interaction of personalities and paused with his finger on the button. Frazer had not given much away. All he had admitted was that K5 was on a general watching brief. There was some concern about the Federal wide hook up of student societies. The enquiry about Vort was noted. That could be the one, though there was nothing on the files to suggest that there was any active conspiracy against the public good.

Fraser had conceded that it was interesting to find that some counter agency was busy trying to rub him out and had advised him to be vigilant, as the department had a lot of training invested in him and couldn't afford reckless waste. As an afterthought, he had thrown in one specific task. There was to be a visit to the region by the Federal Education Minister. More than likely he would do a whistle stop at Picton Polytech. Cain could cover the security angle for the special branch, though without making any personal liaison with the local Public Safety office.

Well, there was time for that. He stubbed the button and began to listen. A cosy female voice posed the question as to whether it was possible to predict the pattern of social interaction between two characters A and B. Easy as breaking an egg, people being consistent in a measure in their basic ration of anxiety, aggression, dominance, introversion and that.

Caution was to be observed in making too rigid a class for A or B. They would have sub-personalities. Which sub-personality was displayed by A would depend on what was being displayed by B at the time.

Cain reckoned that if B was anything like Wanda, A's reaction could be predicted to a millimetre and a good paragraph flowed unheard over his head.

When he returned to focus, she was saying that A could dominate B if he spoke first, talked more and particularly so if he was more intelligent and extraverted.

It figured. B had been getting the greasy end of the pole through the millenia. It didn't even matter whether A was talking sense or not.

He was the natural born politician and B was the sucker who voted him in.

She went on to confirm his diagnosis. 'Where A is indifferent to negative reactions or just does not care, he will not adjust his own behaviour to be accommodating. Though in an extreme case, if he does not compensate B with large enough rewards, B might withdraw from the situation.'

Again she was right on the ball and was going on as if she was A his own self. The only reward he was to get was earache. Like B he should vote with his feet and withdraw to another part of the forest.

Cain shoved down the pause button and carefully filled his pipe. It was dark outside and he went out to look over his balcony. There was no light in the room below and he felt unreasonably irritated. Why couldn't she stay home occasionally and knit a sweater?

He settled down again at his desk, forced himself to concentrate and worked steadily for two hours by the clock. At the end of it, he felt that he had the pre-liminaries all buttoned up and spent ten minutes with isometric drills in case he should turn himself into an intellectual.

Flat on his back with his feet high up the washroom door and his hands clasped behind his neck, he was giving his abdomen its share of the action, when there was a double rap on the outside hatch and he had his first social call.

Art Delacroix was inside looking around for his host before any formal invitation could be given. Finding him at floor level he squatted on his heels and said 'Ah. There you are then. Do you know something?'

Cain relaxed warily ready to roll either way. Delacroix appeared to have two heads and it was very confusing. 'What for instance?'

'I'm a worried man.'

Anybody with two heads had a better than even chance of picking up a problem. Cain lowered his feet, rolled over and stood up for a closer look, His guest was holding a severed head of great classical beauty with short curly hair and long silky eyelashes.

As Delacroix straightened up the left eye closed and opened again in a disembodied wink.

Cain said, 'You have every call to be worried. What did you pull her head off for? Don't you know your own strength?'

Art Delacroix was triumphant, 'There you are you see. Took you in for a start. I tell you, it's uncanny. They have them all over the place in that Cybernetics outfit. Full figure jobs also. Too big to slip out unseen those, but I borrowed this for a close study,'

He plunged his hand in the open neck and drew out a multicore lead. 'This plugs in a desk unit and believe it or not, but she can carry on a rational conversation. More rational than some with all their bits and pieces present and correct.'

'Android development. It's not new. They've been doing humanoid mock ups on robot gear since the turn of the century.'

'Nothing as refined as this. Always backed by a roomful of hardware. They have one there that sits in class. I asked her what she did in her free time and got a very smooth turn off.'

'That's rough. But you can't win them all. The world's full of girls. Try another one. You can't be the only human in the group. Anyway you have to see it from her point of view. Maybe she's going steady with another android.'

Delacroix looked at him over the head, 'You're not serious, Man. Don't you see the implications?'

'Tell me.'

'Two things. How come that a small Polytech like this gets so far ahead? There's a break through here in micro components for the cortex. Actually the brain fills the body cavity and the legs down to the knee, but even then it's tiny compared with what's usually needed.'

'I thought you said you didn't get to take her out?'

Delacroix refused to be sidetracked, 'Secondly and more important they're *independent*. They're not fully programmed. That one was following the course as part of her education. Now I haven't heard about this kind of development and I reckon it would be a very newsy item.'

Cain said slowly, 'I'll go along with that. I don't understand it. Are you sure there wasn't a hook up? Visual range ultra short wave would do it.'

'One reason why I took this head. There's nothing like that. It's self contained.'

'Why hasn't there been a leak before? Other students would notice.'

'Well, I'm a very curious fella. I guess I exaggerated a bit when I said they were all over. I got myself locked in the complex and had a look in the back room. A few of these heads are around though in the lecture theatres.'

'What about the one in class? Somebody else would notice that one.'

'Well she was at the back and I'd moved in real close. She had this tabard with a big zip and being naturally dexterous I had it unravelled a good half metre. Just to run a finger down her spine as a social quip. A bad minute that. Duralumin with little ventilation holes.'

'Then she knows you know?'

'I'm not sure. Not very sensitive to touch.'

'I'd get that head back and forget about it. It's a piece of research they aren't ready to give to the world and you'd be very unpopular if they thought you were going to bring publicity before they were ready. Interesting though. I'm glad you told me.'

'I'll do that thing. But watch who you talk to and investigate with a mine detector before you table a proposition.'

Cain lay on his bed with the light off and a corposant glow from the solar window showing that the town was still taking power from the grid.

There was no sound from the woodwork. Either it was just a prudent fall back device or it was too early for a transmission. Maybe they would wait for deep delta sleep. But how they would know when he was at that stage of the cycle was a mystery. Though if Delacroix was to be believed there was some very sophisticated equipment about.

Usually he could turn off and sleep without trouble but after fifteen minutes in the sack he was still wide awake.

This pick up now would be monitored fairly close. Fifty metres off give or take ten. Not level F with a changing population. Up or down? There were resident staff quarters either way.

Up perhaps? He disconnected a flat electrode which he had stuck on his calf to take a waking signal from the department when there was anything he ought to hear. They could always play it back if he missed it live.

He padded out to the balcony and leaned out, studying the face of the block. Mainly it was dark which was reasonable enough for 0135.

A long way left, on floor F, there was a glow. The floor above seemed universally dark. Over that and three rooms along, there could be a glimmer, but it was difficult to be sure.

He went inside, dressed in a dark turtle neck sweater, dark pants and sneakers, took his laser from its clip and shoved it in his waistband.

On the balcony again, he balanced cautiously on the rail and reached up slowly for the underside of the balcony above. When he had it, he moved his left hand for the outside edge, shifted a centimetre at a time until he could feel a support rail and took a grip. Then with both hands on, he heaved himself aloft.

Gaps between balconies on the same level were not much more than a metre and he traversed until he was below the one he wanted to see. Now it was plain that there was a light on.

He was talking himself into the next move, standing flat against the solar wall in the angle of the balcony, when it went out.

There was the soft scuff of an opening door overhead and a light tread. Movement left. A shadow of darkness on darkness. He was not the only restless spirit about.

This one had traversed left. He let him go and followed underneath. Maybe the monitor had shown that there was no deep breathing coming from his pad and they were checking it out.

Convinced of it, he crossed another gap and looked up for the moving shadow. When it appeared dead ahead coming down to the balcony he was on, he rolled smartly into a ball, covering face and hands.

There was a small hiss of effort as the man found the rail and appeared to slide past it. He was going down a fine flexible ladder, thin as a web in the starlight.

Cain let him go. Saw the tension leave the wires and leaned over the rail. That was room thirty. Why hadn't he gone farther over before going down? He waited for the move across to his own room. There was none.

Then he saw it clear and cursed himself for a fool. The whole conversation with Delacroix could have been picked up. He should have fixed the transmitter with a non op switch. It was Art Delacroix they were after at this point, because of his curiosity on the android issue.

It was time to move. He used the ladder and reached the floor below as the solar hatch opened and a tall, narrow figure slipped inside.

For a second he thought it was Art himself, which would be a turn up for the book. Been to a board meeting with the opposition. All that about the android being a little kite flying to see what he would say.

Then a fine pencil of light moved around the room, picking up the android head on the dressing chest and finally centring on the cybernetics student himself stretched out on top of his trundle bed in bright lemon sleep wear with cossack frogging.

It was a difficult one for Cain. Intervention too early in the sequence would mean that he would never know what was intended. On the other hand leaving it too late might be too late for the dressy sleeper.

The man had taken something from his breast pocket and was.going close.

Cain was in at a run grabbing the wrist and clubbing for the bent head with the butt of his laser.

The man fell forward. Delacroix sat up saying firmly 'I didn't touch her, officer.'

Cain found the bedside light and flicked it on.

They had gotten a complete stranger. Delacroix adjusting himself from his broken phase of rapid eye-movement

47

sleep said, 'Who's this then? What's this fella doing in my bed? And come to think of it, what are you doing here with him, also?'

'Not with him. After him. I saw him nip in here and I followed along to see what he was up to. What's he got there in his hand?'

Delacroix rolled the weight off his thighs and stood up. 'It's a syringe.'

'I guess I should have waited. Then we would have known what he he was up to.'

'*You* would have known. Who knows how receptive I might have been? This is a lot better. He's here, we can ask him.'

With a nice display of controlled power, he picked the man from the bed and carried him into the washroom. There was the sound of running water, a bitter oath and the duo were back. Delacroix had produced a long bone-handled razor, a collector's item, and was shoving it a little way into the man's back in the area of the fourth intercostal.

Hair plastered flat in a dark wet skull cap, lips drawn back a little from an uneven set of yellow teeth, the late visitor was no social catch.

Delacroix said, 'Here he is. A right sunshine elf. Ask him what he was doing with that syringe?'

Glad to have the initiative out of his hands for a spell, Cain said, 'You heard the gentleman. What were you doing with that syringe?'

The outer shell was clearly a fair mirror of what lay below. The voice was flat, catarrhal, non-intellectual. He said, 'Get knotted,' and spat ceremonially to his left.

Delacroix, a jealous housekeeper, said, 'That's not nice,' and moved his razor to a lumbar site without taking it out of its hole.

Spurred forward and seeing the hatch to the balcony still open the man leaped for it with a total mobilization of energy that deserved success.

48

Cain, two metres off, was a fraction late to intercept and followed out at a run. There was not much time for the man to line up on his ladder and he was disorientated by the quick switch from light to dark. He had stopped at the rail hands out searching for contact.

Cain was grabbing for a hold but his questing hands hit the middle of the back. Then he was flailing round for a holdfast to keep himself from following over.

There was a withdrawing yell up the well, a meaty thud and a continuing silence.

Delacroix said, 'The impulsive fool. What did he want to go and do that for?'

For Cain it was becoming a familiar sequence and it was making him nervous. At this rate he was never going to get to ask anybody anything. Fraser wasn't going to like it for a fact.

There was no sudden switch on of lights along the block. The sleepers went right on doing their thing and the few students still batting must have got it muted through the solar wall and put it down to a night-jar.

There was one thing he could do and that was check out the point of origin. He picked up the handy pencil torch and said, 'Have a look at that syringe and tidy up any blood. I'll be right back.'

The ladder made it easier. In three minutes he was on the balcony where he had first seen the light. The solar door was a centimetre ajar and he went in to darkness.

Standing inside he stopped breathing and listened like any beaver. There was a regular drip from the washroom and the knock of a shrinking pipe as the water system settled for a cost saving temperature drop. But there was no human breathing. He sent a fine beam playing round the set.

It was a bigger room than those on floor F. About double overall. There was a bed in an alcove that could

49

be closed off by a green curtain with brass rings sliding on a mahogany pole. There was nobody in it.

The work console was more elaborate than his own. It could well have facilities for monitoring the plants.

He picked up a nest of open shelves and crossed over for a close look. There were some loose leaf folders with a name on the spine. *A Stringer.*

The walking bush himself. It was a nice precise fact to find, like a plum in the bottom of a dish and would do very well to be going on with.

He traversed to the ladder and was down two rungs when he had a better idea.

It was anchored by a two tine grapnel and instead he fed it between two bars and dropped it double. Holding two rungs at a time, very conscious that he couldn't afford to let either one go, he went down one balcony at a time repeating the drill.

Delacroix was waiting to help him over the last sill. 'What do you want the ladder for then?'

'Drop it down there.'

'You know he's not going to have any use for it?'

'Make it look like a prowler having an equipment failure.'

Art Delacroix slapped his forehead with the heel of his hand, 'I guess it's not my time. I'm not smart in the small hours. Good thinking, Metal fatigue. I'll fix it while you take a spell.'

He carried the ladder into his room and took one curved prong at a time. It was tough and the veins stood out in his neck, but he did it with his bare hands, twisting them straight.

Cain said 'Holy Cow. Remind me not to let me get your fingers near my neck. That android bint was surely lucky you only got hold of her toggle.' He wiped the strands with a tissue and dumped the ladder over the sill.

Delacroix said modestly, 'It's just a knack. Saves

carrying a whole lot of tools. Now don't tell me, if you'd rather not, but you have your out-of-the-way skills yourself. That's not standard rig for a science correspondent. How come you were so well placed to stop our friend from interfering with me while I slept?'

'It was pure chance. Your guardian angel was working for you.'

'He's just put a nasty suspicious thought in my head. You wouldn't have been with him by any chance? Shoved him over before he could tell all?'

'Do you think that?'

'Well no. No, I guess not. You have a fine open face. What there is to see of it. Do you want to say what you were doing out there?'

'I'll tell you this much. I found a pick up planted in my wall. I was looking around for a likely site for the monitor. It must have been used when you were in there telling me about the cybernetics wing.'

'So you're not just a straight student. Well who cares? Let's leave it at that. One thing though, if they're so damn particular, they'll try something else. I'll have to be careful.'

'Too right. There won't be anything more tonight though. We'll think around it tomorrow. Use that electronic expertize and rig a little alarm system. I'll send the syringe for analysis. All right?'

'Far from all right, but do what you think best.'

'See you then in the morning.'

'I'll say amen to that.'

Cain wakened to a double rap on his door and a rattle on the latch. He said 'Hold it,' and rolled out to shift the chair he had angled under the pull.

He had gotten three morning callers. Two in olive drab Public Safety rig, with the Picton City flash of a Dolphin rampant on an azure sea, one to the rear looking pleased in his sombre way and the only known quantity in the equation.

'The morning's greetings to you Abe. What's this then? A military coup—'

Before he could answer, the leading hand was walking right in and rather than be trampled flat Cain stood aside. He tried again, 'Will somebody tell me what's going on?'

The spearhead of the force, a high shouldered character with a round cannon ball head, reached the solar hatch, opened it and answered before going through.

'I hoped you could tell me that.'

He went on, leaned briefly over the rail and came in again. 'Billot. Lieutenant Billot and this is Sergeant Suter. Do you know what's down there?'

'A walk or pleasance with a fountain and a black chick pouring water. Has somebody mutilated her urn?'

'Take a look.'

Cain went out and leaned over with Billot joining him at the rail.

He looked straight down, then right. Below the Delacroix balcony there was the white outline of a spreadeagled figure. He said, 'Somebody's been chalking on the sidewalk.'

'That's right. There was a corpse there. We moved it. It looked real nasty. It could have come from this height according to the lab boys. They can calculate a thing like that to within a metre. Compressive strength of materials and all that.'

'That's smart. Saves having to drop people from different levels to get a good match.'

'Right.'

'Some student driven mad by knowledge jumped to his death.'

'Not a student.'

'Who then?'

'Records identified him as a small time criminal,

name of Gilmore. Trained at one time as a medical orderly.'

'He ought to have known better then—compressive strength and that.'

'That's true. One thing that bothers me is a long tear right through his clothing and an incision in his back. Not caused on impact.'

'Lab boys again? They really work at it.'

'The way I see it, he could have been working around these balconies to see what he could pick up, got into a fight with a resident and got pushed over.'

'It must be an occupational hazard.'

Billot led back into the room, 'You didn't hear anything out of the way?'

'Not a thing. I did some work at the desk there, turned in about the midnight hour and slept like any log.'

'I'll just take a look around.'

'Be my guest. You'll have a warrant for that?'

'Does it bother you?'

'Not at all, but we can't have citizens' rights eroded for want of a timely word.'

Suter was working through the picture gallery and had stuck in simple wonder at Wanda.

He said, 'I got a theory Chief. This one could be some kind of deviant and this Gilmore could be putting on a bite. Called here last night for a pay off and Cain threw him out.'

Cain said, 'Right into a force nine gale that blew him away. Now why couldn't your spider man just have an accident like anybody else?'

Billot came out of the wash room with Cain's razor. 'You always shave with this? Those areas you still keep clear?'

'That's right.'

'Okay, Mr Cain. We'll leave it at that. You're sure you can't help?'

'I'd help if I could.'

'All the evidence points to an accident. He was using a ladder and the claws went flat. The lab boys are a little surprised that his weight could have done it.'

'Metal fatigue? Maybe he used it a lot. Built in obsolescence.'

From the door, Billot said 'You're a great theorist, Mr Cain. One day when I have a real tough problem I'll come and talk it over with you.'

'Any time.'

When they had gone Cain straightened his bed, whipped the capsule from its nest and carried it carefully to the verandah. They had enough human speech on tape to keep them happy for a spell, a little birdsong would make an interlude.

He rolled out his trunk and set up his station.

'K5.'

'Go ahead K5.'

'Item for collection. I'd like a fast report on it.'

'Hold.'

There was a half minute wait and he could imagine the reduced night shift in the underground complex which housed the special service, wishing him dead. Another fifteen minutes and they would have been home and dry. He began to fill his pipe and put down the tobacco sack when she spoke again.

'Fifteen hundred is the earliest.'

'That's fine.'

'Take the left hand video booth in the shopping precinct.'

'Check.'

'Anything other?'

'Just for the record, in case I should move suddenly into the spirit world, there's some development in the cybernetics wing here which might repay study. One Stringer, Adrian Stringer is the link man.'

'Is it likely?'

'Is what likely?'

'That you might move out of reach except through the channel of a seance?'

'Could be.'

'I'll tell K1. He might like to work out a knocking code.'

'Don't get carried away. I'd find a very inconvenient time to rattle a chain in your ear. Over and out.'

It was still early for breakfast and he took his pipe to the balcony, shifted the capsule to its usual site and then leaned over to see how his geraniums were faring in all the action.

Two metres off, Christie Maclean's auburn head was tilted back looking up. She was wearing what was basically a pale turquoise leotard with a yellow micro skirt and white sandals with thongs to the calf. Very taut and trim in the morning light.

She said, 'I was hoping to catch you.'

'Okay. I'll go all slack and fall right over.'

'To thank you for the pot plant.'

'My pleasure.'

'What's going on. The janitor here said there'd been an accident.'

'Man overboard. X marks the spot.'

She looked over, then up the cliff face.

'That chalk mark?'

'So they say.'

'That's terrible. Who was it?'

'They think it was a prowler. After your geranium more than likely.'

'I don't understand you. You have a very callous streak. How is it you know so much about it?'

'The experts reckon he fell from about this level and there's been an enquiry all along the floor.'

'They'd obviously ask a man who had a talent for it. If he'd been under your window, I'd have told them.'

'You wouldn't do that.'

'Why not?'

'Look, beautiful as you are from this angle, I'd rather talk to you on the level. What are you doing on Saturday?'

'Why?'

'There's a healthy life outfit that runs a Fell Walk. Have a day in the country with a boiled egg and a tomato sandwich.'

'A new challenge for you. You're going to try pushing somebody off of a cliff?'

'Look Mac. Do me a favour. Be less frivolous. I'll put your name down. Be there with your hair in a braid and your victuals in a red hanky.'

'Okay. I guess a group like that needs protection. I'll pack my surgical scissors.'

'Spoken like the chief's own daughter. They'll come in to cut sprigs of *edelweiss* at the snowline.'

'Actually, you won't have to push people. They'll be jumping off to get away from the sound of your voice. I must be out of my mind.'

Reckoning it was as good a last word for her to have as any, Cain waved and went in.

He was early in the diner, but Art Delacroix had beaten him to it. Using his elbows and stamping on a couple of feet, he came out of the ruck with ninety per cent of his choices and made his way across.

'How did it go? You had a visit?'

'Surely. They were okay. They seemed to have it all buttoned up. Small time operator with a record. Open and shut case.'

'The tall guy, Billot wanted to see my razor.'

'That's right. He looked at my automatic. The other one, I'd stuffed in that android head.'

'Good thinking.'

'Dodgy though. The sergeant picked it up. Asked what I'd done with the body. He was saying that student accommodation ought to be on the vice squad list.'

'Watch how you go today in your department. Stay with the crowd.'

'I'll do that.'

Cain had time to spare and made a detour to the recreation block to sign up for the trip. Looking up the list, he saw that Brigitta Ross had added her name and next to it was Delacroix himself. There were thirty takers. Three others from his own course, seven from Cybernetics and the rest a random scatter across the board. Maybe he ought to get Fraser to lay on a gunship to patrol the route.

The morning session was a little rough. Stringer was there operating the actualizer, giving nothing away. The lecturer on the closed circuit link was a young man with a beaky nose and a high pitched, quick fire delivery. He covered a lot of ground. Like Cleator he was working on A and B and B was not doing well.

There was a lengthy digression on the underlying dynamics of looking at one's neighbour and Delacroix was missing some valuable info.

Looking had its reward if it was responded to by a smiling face and it was found that electrical activity in the brain was increased by a good Look.

When A was ready to crack off into speech, he looked away from B, took a few brief peeks in mid flow and then at the end of the *spiel* latched right on to B with a prolonged visual blast, no doubt to check that he was still all systems go and not nodding off.

If at this point B looked away, he had thrown in the towel. A could trample all over his psyche and rush him into any proposition.

The lecturer in his holographic web was bombproof anyway. The fair girl who had slept through the previous session was looking round uneasily as though she had recognized herself as a natural B.

Cain found he was staring fixedly at Stringer. That one was impassive, hands relaxed on his console, eyes unfocused, directed to a point half a metre over the heads of the back row.

The text flowed on with the wretched B falling into the error that if he couldn't see A, A couldn't see him and covering his face with his hands. Particularly if he had a guilty secret.

Stringer made no move to follow the pattern. No doubt he had heard it all before and had techniques of his own to beat the rap.

The second stint of the morning was in the experimental lab. Each had a measured learning task with a teaching machine and a sequence of nonsense items.

Stringer moved among his flock with the encouraging word and finally gravitated to a point behind Cain's chair.

'You're doing well with that. Scoring high. Have you used this kind of apparatus before?'

'Not for some years. General science courses way back.'

'Of course. I see from your profile you were working with actualities on the science side. Thinking of changing your field?'

'Not really. Just interest. I like to have the background jargon. Information has a way of being useful.'

'You were at our meeting the other night.'

Cain worked through another six frames and made a full score.

'That's so.'

'No comment?'

'Not at this stage.'

'Just interest?'

'Right. The founding father used to work here, I believe?'

'Yes. A great man. Retired now, but still one of the best political thinkers of the age.'

'Very frustrating for him. We have a good political system. Democratic, stable, no depressed peasantry shaking the railings and asking for bread.'

'There's more to it than bread. We need a system that matches the potential of the twenty-first century mind.'

'Whose twenty-first century mind for instance?'

'I'll talk to you again. I see you're down for the trip at the weekend. Maybe we can clear up your doubts . . . '

'We can surely try.'

CHAPTER FOUR

Skilled though he was in the theories of eye contact, having sat in on the course for five gruelling years, Stringer had trouble with his visitor. The man's face was as mobile as that of a bland, stone carved Buddha and the pale, expressionless eyes never left his face.

He was sitting in the office when Stringer went in to catch up with a little paper work in the dead mid afternoon period. He said 'Langton, George Langton. Can I talk to you here?'

Stringer closed the door and settled himself in his desk. Knowing that everybody had one, he asked civilly, 'What's your problem?'

'I don't have one. You have one and I'm here to help you with it.'

'That's friendly.'

'I'll come right to the point. You have a man called Cain on your books. He could be dangerous to you.'

'I know all about Cain. He's under observation.'

'Tell me. Was Gilmore trying to get him when he fell off his ladder?'

'Why should I know that?'

'I know he was one of the hatchet men in your organization and he went on his mission from your room.'

'Whose side are you on?'

'Your side, Mr Stringer. Your side. Have no fear, I have no contact with Public Safety either Federal or local. Quite the reverse. We have a mutual interest in finding out why Cain is here and in putting him away.'

'A vendetta?'

'You could say that. He has been a nuisance to me.'

'Having said so much, surely you can tell me what your interest is?'

'Perhaps I will. Your organization, as I understand it, has global ambitions. You have no narrow, nationalist limitations. Money would be useful to you wherever it came from?'

'That is so.'

'How would you react if I told you that Southern Hem could be generous? We have never been blinded by the democratic myth. Your programme is more in line with our political thinking than that of the Atlantic Federation.'

'Our?'

'There you are you see. In my frank, open way, I have shown my interest.'

'But why come to me? This is only a minor branch of the movement.'

'I think not, Mr Stringer. You are not matching openness with openness. Professor Vort is more often in touch with this unit than any other and you have an important project in hand at the moment. Could that be why Cain is here?'

'What project do you have in mind?'

'Again I'll put my cards on the table. I believe it has to do with Eisenberg's visit. The exact details we do not know.'

'But you're doing all right.'

'We like to know what goes on and we have many agents in the field. An alliance would bring advantages.'

'To you or to us?'

'It would be mutual.'

'I can see that a period of unrest in the Federation would leave Southern Hem with a clear field. Are you aiming to take over?'

'A world state? Communication techniques are not

ready for it. Southern Hem is big enough. But a government we could be comfortable with would be a step forward.'

Stringer left his desk and walked to the window. The exercise seemed to do him good and he came to a decision. He said, 'We had a tip from another group that Cain might be an agent. His room is monitored. The record so far seems to confirm it. Gilmore was going for his neighbour who picked up information we were not ready to release. You are saying that Cain is an agent. Therefore it's unlikely that Gilmore had a straight accident.'

'Very quick. Very sound deduction. I can see that we shall get on very well.'

'You won't have come here without something definite in mind. Do you aim to tell me what it is?'

'I want to meet Professor Vort and put a proposition to him.'

'That could be arranged. Your credentials would have to be checked.'

'Of course. That is not difficult. There is a consulate in Picton City. The consul will give you all the assurance you need. I will meet you there.'

'I am well known here. I can't go visiting the Southern Hem Consulate.'

'It is in the office development over the shopping precinct. There is a travel agency below it. Ask for brochures on Gabon and Loanda.'

'When?'

'Tomorrow afternoon. Say fifteen hundred?'

'Very well.'

Langton rose to his feet and was seen to be shorter than he looked sitting down. At the door, he said, 'I am sure you will not regret your decision. Until tomorrow then, Mr Stringer.'

Left alone Adrian Stringer roamed thoughtfully round his office. It was disturbing to be an open book even to a self-styled ally. First priority was to identify the leak. Mentally he checked over the inner wheel of the Vorticist cell. Mainly they were permanent staff at the Polytech like himself. Mentzoni from the Language Division. Pollitt from Graphics, Nelson and O'Connell from Cybernetics. They were sound enough.

He went through the three liaison members from the town. Pitman from the Consolidated Trades Council, a natural born revolutionary, he would have no dealing with a reactionary government like Southern Hem. There was Rouse who always argued the toss, a barrack room lawyer if ever there was one, but sold solid on the programme. He wouldn't have the nerve for it. Nor would the last member of the executive committee Joe Foden.

No, there was nothing there. It had to be an outsider who had gotten real close and had some sophisticated equipment backing him up. The Southern Hem outfit itself. Nelson was the man to sort that out. He could get some of his experts busy on it. Right away. With Eisenberg's visit due in three days, they should close the gap. Operate from strength in any deal there was with Langton.

He called on the internal video and got Carl Nelson first crack out of the bag.

'Busy, Carl?'

'You could say that,' Nelson's contact lenses were in a cross light and he looked like an intelligent horse lit from the inside.

'I'd like five minutes of your time. It's important.'

'Okay. I'll be right over.'

A minute early at the tryst, Robert Cain kept himself out of sight in the crowded central square of the precinct.

He saw Stringer's head move through the press like a mobile bush and had a problem. It would be nice to know what a Vorticist did in his free time. But his own schedule was strict. He had seen a girl in a tomato tabard take up the end booth and he had to be next with the video.

He gave her thirty seconds and hove to outside, tapping on the glass and saying, 'Why don't you write him a letter?'

She turned her back in a mime of indignation, completed her call and stalked out saying 'Some people have no manners.'

Cain made a play with the auto directory, dialling the name Pontius Pilate. The indicator flashed up 'No current number listed.'

He had found a pea sized capsule on the parcel tray and slipped it in his pocket.

Through the glass, he could see Stringer's head going through a swing door.

He dialled a random number and got an oldster with a missing front tooth who looked annoyed and went off on a private piece of gobbledegook which was inaudible, because Cain was saving his money and had not completed the hook up. But he went through the motions, nodded intelligently and said, 'It will all be one on the last day.' Then he pulled the plug and crossed the square to see what Stringer was at.

Planning a vacation seemingly. The door he had used served the premises of the Golden Highway Travel Bureau and if the visual presentation was to be believed, every lucky traveller with the firm got a bronzed nymph wearing a navel jewel to rub on his sun oil.

It was worth an enquiry and Cain pushed open the door and let himself in.

Most of the floor area was taken up with exotic pot plants, giving the set a hot house, jungle flavour. Small birds with brilliant plumage were nipping about in free flight. A long counter with high stools and a foot rail for clients ran along one wall. Three girls in leopard skins to further the company image were leaning over the bar answering queries.

The other long wall was divided into booths where actualizers were creating 3-D samples of far away places, so that the customer could try it out without leaving Picton City.

Cain walked the length of the display. At the end, there was a room divider of yellow pine spars and bougainvillia growing from a trough. An opening left was sign posted to wash rooms for either sex, a thoughtful provision in case the excitement should prove too much. On the right it said Staff Only, an escape route for the leopards.

There was no sign of Stringer. Cain reclined in a chair under a palm tree and helped himself to a portfolio on Cambodia. Even the glossy presentation could not entirely destroy the charm of the place. He was looking at a double spread of Angkor Wat when a warm voice breathed in his ear, 'Can I do anything for you?' and he had gotten a spare leopard at his elbow.

'If I say, "Not a thing" take it in a pure commercial sense. Just window shopping. Unless you'd crouch at my side and turn the pages.'

'Well, just say if there's anything.'

She roamed off through the forest and Cain gave himself another five minutes by his watch.

There was still no sign of Stringer. He made another circuit of the store and went out into the square.

It was another ten minutes before Stringer's ball of fuzz appeared through the hatch and he was scratching it reflectively as though a bird of paradise had nested in it. Langton had established an identity. It was all as he said. He had gone farther. As a test of good faith he had undertaken to rub out Cain or Delacroix or both before the end of the week leaving the choice fraternally to Stringer himself.

Stringer had said modestly that one would be enough to be going on with and had chosen Delacroix as the immediate danger. He had stipulated that it should be off the campus. Too many deaths would bring more attention than they wanted at this point in time.

In return he had agreed to talk to Vort and arrange a meeting.

On balance, the new factor seemed okay. Extra help could be useful. Vort could assess that and see how far he wanted to go. They could watch developments. Let Langton think he was an equal partner and be ready to dump him when his usefulness was over. After all, he was out on a limb. A call to the right quarters could get him put away with the Vorticists getting a medal as watchdogs of the common weal.

He stopped scratching his head and turned his steps towards the Polytech, conscious that he had put in another good afternoon for the cause and turning his mental engine to the details of the Eisenberg exercise. He even began to hum a little tune.

Cain watched him out of sight and took the escalator to the next floor of the complex.

There was a Chinese Grill Room at the stairhead, a broad circulation space with an outcrop that overhung the street and rows of yellow settles so that a contemplative man could sit and watch the human tide.

He leaned out to catch the sun on his face, filled his pipe, watched for a spell and concluded a crowd was a crowd was a crowd.

There was no difference. He could have been in Bangkok or any one of the Golden Highway's distant cities. Give or take a shade or two in skin colour, they were all on the same basic ploy. Out on a foray from the home base. New socks for Junior, food for the evening meal, a plastic cat for the window sill. Essential human business of a non-political nature. Stringer must be out of his tiny mind to think they would give two damns in hell for his programme. Or anybody else's.

They had it made in security. Well dressed, well fed,

66

reasonably housed, free from pain, they wanted tomorrow to be like today only more so.

He turned his back to the rail and examined the inside scene. It was difficult to work out where the travel bureau lay in relation to the floor he was on.

On a rough calculation, he had two choices and he walked over to look closely at the frontage. One was a finance house specialising in property deals. 'Bricks and mortar are here when you're gone. You know it makes sense.'

Next door was a more discreet enterprise and he had to search for a label. He found it engraved on the ground glass of the door itself. There was a helix like an unwinding DNA spiral with the legend in Condensed Gothic— Southern Hemisphere Government. Consulate Forty-one. Dr A. V. Lyer.

It was enough to be going on with. Like Stringer he turned his steps for home.

Langton, who had been watching him on a scanner in the consul's private room, said, 'I have a bad feeling about Cain. Stringer underestimates the danger. They are very naïve. I doubt that we shall gain much from this venture. But we shall see. Meanwhile Cain should be dealt with. He is not clever, but lucky, and that is worse.'

Lyer, a Levantine with full lips and a round swarthy face said, 'I am sure you are right, George. Make it as soon as possible. He can know nothing but even suspicion is too much. Do you need extra men?'

'I think not. Donovan has free access to the campus. He can work on it right away.'

Cain went methodically to work, moved the pick up to his verandah, closed the door and broke open the new capsule. Its micro spool slotted home in the base of his multi-purpose razor, which he plugged in to his battered trunk.

67

It was a quiet voice and he had to put his ear flat to the fabric to hear it all.

The analysts had worked fast. The drug from the hypo was on the restricted list but they reckoned it had been made up at some local dispensary. It was not a killer. The effect would be total on the higher nerve centres for a matter of minutes and then it would break down leaving no trace. Ideal to immobilize a subject until some other action could be taken. It was also useful to plant hypnotic suggestion. Any instruction given during the operative period would not register on the conscious mind, but would be followed out when the patient was back on circuit. The hypo itself was normal medical service issue and was one of a batch supplied to the Picton City Public Health Department. From there it could have been routed to the Polytech Medical Unit which drew its stores from the city pool.

Cain went into reverse and dismantled the gear, replaced the pick up, crushed the micro tape between his fingers and sluiced it away in his wash bowl.

That figured. Gilmore would have two options. He could either drag Delacroix to the balcony and shove him over or simply tell him to do it for himself when he woke up. Probably that one. Two or three minutes would be enough for him to get the hell out of it and watch the action from a distance.

Gilmore as a one time medical orderly could have picked up the syringe any place. On the other hand it could have come from Christie Maclean's store cupboard. Via Donovan even. A regular citizen would not carry a bijou transmitter in his topcoat. Maybe he was one of Stringer's outside links?

Where did that put the girl? Not good either way. A dupe or a very devious item.

He went next door to see how Delacroix was making out and found him hunched over his pianolo reinforcing the day's hand-out of technical sludge. He could not look pale, but he could look weary and he flapped his hand in sombre greeting. 'This is beginning to give me a pain in my gut. There's a bad slant to it. You'd swear they believed they were engineering people. I don't think it's intended, but it comes out all the time. They want to see androids accepted with voting rights and community status.'

'It's a legitimate point. If they can mock up a girl well enough to confuse an *afficionado* like yourself and give her a free wheeling brain pack that can take in information for its own use, they've made an individual. Enough of them would make a lobby on robotic rights. Vote on the price of mineral ores like on the price of butter or whatever.'

'You're not serious?'

'Let's face it, the human crop motivates on a few simple drives. Shelter, food, sex, status if you like. These monkeys could operate on three out of four. What's the difference?'

'That's sour.'

'One thing's for sure, they'd have the edge on you and me in the long term. They'd have a life span in centuries. Indefinite even, given a good maintenance service. Which brings me to a point. I reckon we should work a watch system around here. For a time anyway. Cover the hours from midnight to first light.'

'You think they'll try again?'

'Very likely.'

'How do we work that?'

Cain examined the party wall, put his ear to it and tapped around with his knuckles. In the corner beside the street door he found what he was looking for.

'There's a main beam here. A divider butts onto that. This panel makes the back wall of my closet. I'll cut out a flap low down, big enough to get through. Fix a scanning beam on the verandah and whoever's awake can be through to sort it out before they get through the hatch.'

'Okay.'

'I'll do it right away and we can start tonight. Zero to three or three to six?'

'I'm easy.'

'Change about. Tonight I'll take until three. Tomorrow you.'

'Whatever you say, but I don't fancy it for a long haul. I like my sleep.'

No stranger to long vigils, Cain was nevertheless getting edgy at 0300. The whole complex was still as any grave. It was two hours since a faint step in the corridor had signalled the last late returner to floor F. He was coming round to the view that they would go another way to work. After Gilmore, they wouldn't want publicity on the site.

He debated whether or not to waken Delacroix. But that decided him. For himself he would have taken a chance and packed it in. With another one at risk he couldn't do it without a conference. He rolled quietly out of the sack and crawled through the hole into the next apartment.

There was moonlight from the solar wall. Art Delacroix woke at a touch and was up like a released spring grabbing for a hold. One who learned fast from experience.

Cain hissed, 'Steady. Your hour has struck.'

'Oh, it's you. That's what I was afraid of. Anything going on?'

'Not a mouse stirring.'

'That's what I like to hear.'

'You're awake?'

'Surely I'm awake. Don't worry. I'll stay that way.'

'Then I'll turn in.'

Cain crawled away through his bolt hole, rolled into bed and took thirty seconds to drift into stage one sleep.

Less used to the rigours of the military life, Art Delacroix roamed moodily round his apartment.

He took a drink from his flask, sat at his desk, then lay down again with his hands behind his head.

Thinking about androids he saw that there was one parameter they had left out of the equation. Emotion. There was nothing yet that suggested they could build in anything resembling human emotion. However smart, the tin bastards wouldn't be pleased that they were up and about and part of the scene. Or would they?

It bothered him and he got up again, padded over to the hole and looked through to see if Cain was still awake.

The door of the closet was open and there was enough light to see the figure on the bed. Not easily though. There was a quiver on the image as though he was looking at it over the heat of an open fire.

Crawling farther in he identified the source. A metre from the side of the bed, a grey pipe was standing a hand's breadth through the parquet and giving off a steady stream of pale grey effluent that was already seeping towards the hole.

Even as he watched a second pipe broke surface beside it.

Holding his breath, he was through and beside the sleeper.

Cain's reaction was instantaneous and he was sitting up looking for a target with his laser.

Delacroix, hand over his mouth and nose pointed in dumb show, whipped back the way he had come.

Cain followed and fitted the loose panel. When it was done, he said 'Nice work. That was close. So much for vigilance. What made you take a look?'

'Just seeing if you were awake. I had a thought about androids.'

'I'll hear it another time.'

'What do we do now?'

'Wait. Two tubes there. They'll fill the room, then clear it. After that we can expect a visitor.'

'Doesn't that Scottish bint live under you?'

The thought had already crossed Cain's mind with a bitter self jibe. It had not taken long for her to pass on the information that he was a card holder in the security forces.

On the other hand, he could still see her face on the walkway when she was all set to call a gendarme. If that was an act, there was no honesty anywhere to be found. And for that matter, to be fair, he was already picked out for attention. This sequence need not stem from anything she had done.

So where did that leave her? Not proven at the least count.

He said suddenly. 'Hang on here, keep out of line from the window. I'll take a look downstairs. Give me fifteen minutes and if I don't show up ring Billot.'

'Why don't we just ring Billot anyway? He'd like to see that little pipe sticking out of your floor.'

'And he'd get fresh ideas about Gilmore. You'd be wired for sound on a veracity probe in five minutes flat. Get you two years for minor homicide. Just make an anonymous call. Say you think there's a prowler on floor F.'

'In a nervous falsetto?'

'Right.'

Cain used the emergency stairway, a narrow spiral beside the elevator trunk, judging that the whine of a moving cage coming down would be heard all over the floor.

Outside Christie Maclean's hatch he stopped and put his ear to the panel. There was a faint rhythmic beat. They had gotten to the extraction phase.

Fingertips spread he tried to slide the door. It was locked. A fine probe from the butt of his laser fed delicately into the lock and he felt the wards move over.

He counted ten, emptying his mind and concentrating on the room, until he had a picture of it like a projection on the blank surface. Then he slid back the hatch with his left hand and stepped through in one smooth, continuous action.

Physical detail slipped into place as though the flat image had simply deepened into 3-D.

Three human elements not on the rough draft stood out in the composition. Two were kneeling on the floor watching the dials of a small rotary pump unit. The owner of the pad was lying on her back on her bed in a short magenta shift with her ringlet across her throat like a pale sepia rope and appeared to be asleep.

Two heads whipped round smartly to watch him in and the left hand marker with a spreading forehead and a small vicious mouth continued his move in an athletic frog jump with a hand going for an inside pocket.

Cain shot once and the laser was lined up again on the second man who stayed rock still.

There was a split second pause with the jumper still in flight and a crash as he came to an uncontrolled landing all over Christie Maclean's dressing chest. An elegant phial rolled deliberately to the edge, dropped off and broke on the floor with a whip crack. The air change perked up as though blowing straight from an old world garden.

The man beside the pump remained still as a carving, eyes watchful. Christie Maclean went right on sleeping and Cain suddenly began to feel more cheerful. A normal householder would surely have sat up asking to be told who was interfering with her cosmetics. It could just be that she was not in on the act.

On the other hand she must have known one or other of the visitors to let them get close. One was Cyril for a gold clock.

The survivor was fair, with a big chin and tufty sideburns. Probably thirty-five, but would look younger in a good light.

Cain said, 'Stand up, Cyril, and he counted.'

It was all true. The eyes looked surprised before they

reverted to their concentrated stare. Cyril Donovan rose to his feet keeping his hands prudently in view. There was a good two metres of him, nicely muscled, giving off a professional charm that might have dazzled even Delacroix's android. By and large it was a pity he had not been the one to try for glory.

Donovan said, 'So what are you going to do about it?' and although the text was contentious, the voice was well modulated and Cain recognized it might be like spooned honey to the sleeping girl. 'That's a stupid question from you.'

The pump sucked dry and switched itself out. Donovan's eyes flickered towards it.

Cain went on, 'For a start you can pack up this gear and plug those holes in my floor. The janitor might think I was some kind of deviant. And just reflect that I'm not particular. I'd as soon you joined your little bald buddy as not.'

'Suppose I say no?'

'You're a great one for open ended questions, Cyril.'

Cain shifted his aim and fired a split second burst to the back of Donovan's left hand.

It triggered a stream of profanity as though he had breached a dyke, but Donovan moved smartly to the chore and began packing the gear into a neat purpose-built valise.

Cain backed off to the video and shifted call buttons with his left hand. He skipped the picture and made do with a voice link.

Delacroix said, 'Are you all right? I was counting down for a call.'

'I'm all right. I'm talking to Cyril here. He's fixing up the mess. I'll be back in about ten minutes. Earlier if he's real deft. Over and out.'

Still using his left hand he felt inside the bald man's jacket and helped himself to a compact hand gun.

Donovan had the pipes stowed and was holding two cylindrical plugs that had been reamed out.

'I'll need the table over here to fix these in.'

They carried it between them, Cain using his left hand. He could see that Donovan was hoping to shift the weight and catch him off balance, but it would take a cold nerve and it was a bad time of day for heroic gestures. To encourage him he said, 'Try it, Cyril. Have a go. Get yourself a posthumous Purple Heart.'

'You've got a big mouth, Cain. I can wait my turn.'

'Tell me, does our sleeping medical friend know about your spare time hobbies?'

'You'll have to find out won't you?'

'I'll do that. I just wondered if she'd be around to poke grapes through the bars on visiting days or whether she'd be pacing her own cell in a drab smock.'

Donovan shoved the plugs home and jumped down. 'What now?'

'You're free as a bird. Pick up the casualty and go away. Leave the grip, I always wanted a home gas chamber outfit.'

'You'll regret this.'

'I'd regret it more if I'd found myself dead.' He opened the door and stood aside to let Donovan out.

From the threshold, he watched him to the stair head. Getting rid of a body would keep his mind off sin for an hour or two.

The air in the room still carried a rich pollen cloud and it reminded him of the silent partner. He straightened her dressing chest, dumped the broken phial in the disposal chute and sat on the edge of the bed. She was still at it, lips slightly open showing a nice even set of white teeth, eyelashes in even arcs. Maybe for the sleeper, there was democracy in the sleeping state, all coming to the same rhythm, the good, the bad, the clever and the dull. But for the observer there was a difference. She was still in a very superior league.

He picked up the nearest wrist and felt the pulse. Slowish but strong and steady. They had used a variant of the knock out drop. But how administered? Surely she was not so besotted with the man that she would let Cyril get close with a hypo?

The hand was on the cold side so he rolled her to the far edge, eased down the covers and rolled her into the sack.

It seemed an anti climax, but there was nothing else to be done.

There had been a lot of traffic in the corridor so he called Delacroix again. 'All through here. I'm coming up. I'll use the balcony. Just in case you might start any fancy action with that razor.'

Leaning out to water the geranium on the basis that it would be unfair to work off pique on an innocent party, Cain came near to pouring a generous half litre on the girl herself.

She was standing on her balcony in her sea horse bra and triangular briefs drawing deep breaths, hands shoulder high and straight out like a sleep walker.

Cain said, 'That's the way, Mac. A healthy mind in a healthy body. Sing a morning song, if you like, and for a fee I'll join in with the chorus.'

'Oh it's you.'

'And who else would you expect over your head?'

'Go away.'

'Did you have a late night then? Liverish? Cyril take you on the town?'

'Are you a necromancer or something?'

'That's a very filthy jibe in the clear morning light.'

'Actually we came home early. I was tired and I went to bed. I don't even remember getting into it and another funny thing I must have broken a perfume jar and cleared it away and I don't remember that either.'

'Cyril must have been feeding you strong liquor for a sinister end.'

'Trust you to think of that. He's not devious like some.'

'Anybody called Cyril would have to be devious. Probably came back when you were asleep and broke your bottle. If he has his hand in a bandage, he cut it on the glass. Serve him right too.'

'I don't think I could stand you for a whole day. I'll have to think very carefully about Saturday.'

'Think how fond I am of your geranium. That can't be bad can it?'

A distant chiming clock sounded the hour and she started like a spirit at cock crow. 'Now I'm going to be late. This is going to be one of those days.'

She disappeared with a pleasing long-legged action and he was left to empty his can on the hanging basket.

It was a long day and Cain felt he was tackling it with a divided mind.

Eisenberg's visit was scheduled for the next day and there were preparations being made. Extra cleaning staff had been whistled in and some classes were grouped together to leave clear rooms.

Delacroix came through the connecting hatch after the evening meal and told the same tale. Except that he had another angle.

'There's something brewing there in Cybernetics. The practical labs were closed all day and half the staff were missing.'

'Cooking up a demonstration for the Minister. Your girl's going to do a bump and grind routine as a party piece.'

'He's visiting the section. We were told that. No classes after eleven hundred. It's the star unit at Picton.'

Cain searched his desk for the weekly campus newsheet and the detail of the tour was listed for all interested parties, together with a full front mug shot of Eisenberg himself. Dark, of indeterminate age, a face indeed that would not alter much between thirty and sixty.

The text said he was a solitary man, dedicated to politics, without wife or close ties and spent a lot of time at a secluded villa in a Welsh valley.

Cain tore out the picture and put it in his pocket. He said, 'It's time we stopped being at the receiving end of everybody's interest. We'll go and take a look at that Cybernetics wing.'

'Now? They'll still be working.'

'Not now. Later on. Now we can get a little sleep. I'll waken you about midnight. That is if you want to come.'

'Surely I want to come. I'm very curious.'

'Can you use one of these?'—Cain opened a drawer and took out his spare laser.

'Fine. That evens things up a little.'

'See you, then.'

CHAPTER FIVE

Art Delacroix led through the maze of the Cybernetics Section and came to a halt at a plain double leaf door marked *Staff Only*.

He was right on one count, the model heads on their mounts were a macabre addition to the decor. Eyes and teeth catching what little light there was, they seemed to be watching the action like so many ghouls.

Cain took two minutes with the lock and Delacroix roamed around closing eyes like a mortician.

Inside there was pitch darkness and no external window. Cain found the switch and a long strip light came on.

There was not much to see. It was a regular preparation room; work desks for staff; a technician's assembly spread filling one wall with an overhead rail carrying a block and tackle for lifting heavy gear; two glass cubicles for lecturers to hook up on the closed circuit actualizer net; a head of Nefertiti used as a paper weight on one of the larger desks.

'Where's your girl, then?'

'Not here for a fact.'

There was a wash room with a line of white lab coats and named lockers, a small lounge area with coffee tables and reclining chairs and a scatter of scientific journals.

Cain stood in the centre of the main room and looked around. If there was an ongoing door in regular use, the disposition of furniture ought to be a guide. Or the lifting gear. They would need to move completed work in and out.

The rail went the length of the work bench and had two off shoots with a shunting system to switch direction. One circled the room on an oval loop. One made an S crossing and butted on to the facing wall.

He followed it over and looked at the floor. There were scuff marks right up to the wall.

Delacroix had been examining a switch panel on the work bench. He said 'I've identified everything but one. That's got a fancy lock. Needs your little gizmo.'

Cain worked on it and heard the click over his shoulder as a section of wall began to slide away and Delacroix's 'Holy Cow. Only look at that. There she is, too.'

It was like lifting a stone and finding a termite colony.

Light from the room they were in cut a swathe through a waxworks show. Figures standing in the dark waiting for resurrection. And the light was doing that thing. Those in its path were stirring into life, heads turning towards the open door.

Cain said, 'It's the light. Phototropic. Switch it off.'

'Stay in the dark with that bunch? Are you crazy?'

'Those at the back aren't moving. It must take a fair light level to switch them on. I'll use the torch.'

Delacroix thumbed over the switch and Cain sent a narrow pencil beam through the hatch. He was right, forward movement had stopped.

He spotlighted a single face and its owner turned slowly into the beam convinced that dawn was at hand.

'There must be fifty. Why would they want that many?—' Delacroix stayed in the doorway, reluctant to move. Cain said, 'I'll send your friend out. Tell her you have ways and means of making her talk and see what she has to say.'

She was certainly a honey. Put into store in a black sweater with a bright yellow band at the midriff, a suede necklace carrying a silver heart and a heavily pleated check skirt, she was ready for the next day's stint at culture's coal face.

She followed the light into the main room, passing within a centimetre of Delacroix without taking her eyes off the pencil beam.

Cain said, 'Close the door behind me and put the light on. Maybe with all round stimulation she'll be more responsive.'

'Do you have to go in there? I've got a feeling they could turn nasty.'

'I shan't take long. Just a quick look at the faces. Maybe it's going to make some sense.'

'Well keep holding that torch, if I come in after you I want to know who's who.'

With his back to the closed door Cain felt a crawl of nerves along the inside of his throat. Telling himself that they were machines and he held the switch was no help. Each face, held momentarily in the light, was human enough to have its niche in the social fabric. They were at least as real as the crowd he had watched in Picton's shopping precinct.

He worked round the first group. They were all representative student types dressed in the current style, knitwear and suede with thonged sandals to the calf for the girls, slacks and linen bush jackets for the men.

Behind them was a more mature group and as he went on he could see that someone had made a cross section of the whole community by age and sex. They had a useful crowd of extras for any occasion. If there was a financial angle in it, they could cover costs by hiring the whole lot to any actualities studio. So long as they weren't asked to strip off to their perforated duralumin, they'd go like a bomb.

In fact when you got right down to it, the whole actualities field could be taken over by androids. Then a little extension to the audience end and the cycle was complete. Androids imitating human behaviour for the benefit of androids imitating human behaviour by watching androids imitating human behaviour.

His torch flicked to the back row and centred on a dark familiar face and he searched in his pocket for the cutting about Eisenberg.

There was no doubt about it. Down to a mole at the corner of his mouth, it was a replica of the Minister.

Surprise made Cain slow to shift the beam and the man was perking up by the second, ready to propose a motion or move an amendment at the drop of a paper clip.

Cain backed off, reached the hatch and slipped through without letting in enough light to start a demo. He heard the android girl say, 'You have no right to be in this part of the unit. I have no intention of answering any of your questions.'

So they had another problem. As soon as she was unpacked for the morning's work, she was likely to start sounding off about having been interfered with in the small hours.

Under the nearest desk was a large plastic tape bin, empty and ready for the next day's take. He picked it out and before she realized the full depths to which a human being would go, he had stepped smartly up and dropped it over her head.

All movement stopped. She was a lay figure.

Cain said, 'Here's some practical course work. Find her memory banks and erase the last ten minutes. Then we'll shove her back in store and go home. They've got a replica of Eisenberg in there and we can't afford to have the metal bint get chatty about this visit.'

Delacroix rolled up her jumper and exposed a neat midriff with an oval panel and an indented locking stud in the navel. He found a tool kit on the bench and went to work.

A fist size plug-in unit was first out of the cavity and Cain had to move in to catch her as she went limp. He said, 'That's major surgery. Maybe we should have used an anaesthetic.'

'This is it. Data acquisition network primary recording. They replay in coded form to the higher centres. A lot of background learning can be fed in direct to this point. It makes you think. Cuts out a lot of trial and error. We'd all be better with one.'

'Can you fix it?'

'I think so. I could even feed in a little confusion. Like, "Beard is beautiful. When you see a man with a beard he is your friend. Follow him like a dog and obey his every whim".'

'Just a straight job will be fine. Make it real fast, she's a well built girl.'

Delacroix was five minutes by the clock and Cain was beginning to think they should have put her on a slab.

When the unit went in, she straightened slowly and took her own weight. With the main light off, he used the torch to guide her to the hatch and returned her to her place in the silent crowd.

Delacroix said, 'A lot of these faces seem familiar. I guess they must have had them in the lecture groups from time to time to try them out.'

It was a remark that went on in Cain's head until they were almost home. Then he said, 'Wait a minute. If they made a replica of Eisenberg, those figures could be replicas of other people. Maybe you've seen the real ones.'

'Not the girl. That was the one.'

'That time it was. Another day you might have had the real one.'

'That would have been better.'

'Next time get her name and we'll do a little checking. With all their fancy equipment they could have made sure that the real one was not going to turn up and start a scene.'

'What about tomorrow?'

'There's a time scheme for Eisenberg's visit. I want him in sight from the minute he gets on the premises. I'll be around up to the point where he reaches Cybernetics.

You cover it from there. I take it they'll allow students in the section?'

'Surely. He's supposed to look at some practical work. I can get in on that.'

'If you notice anything out of the way, come right out and find me.'

'What am I looking for?'

'I don't know. Nothing makes much sense at this stage.'

'You can say that again.'

As the day wore on, Cain became convinced he was on the wrong tack. Eisenberg and two support files from his department appeared on schedule, smiled falsely for an actualizer crew and pushed off on tour with the Polytech Director and a mixed bag of departmental heads.

At one point Cain infiltrated close enough to hear a little of the philosophic hand-out. Eisenberg was saying in that authoritative tone used by administrators to push conviction against the tide of reason, 'Students should be conditioned to freedom of choice and personal responsibility rather than trained for conformity to a discipline. We must move towards more democratic control where students have a decision in the content of the courses they follow.'

Reply was lost as the group moved on, but nods and significant looks suggested that one and all reckoned he had touched the living heart of their problem with a needle.

It was a vote catcher all right for the student body, but one outside the circle, with no subsidy to lose by disagreement, could see a flaw or two. A patient on an operating table for instance would be glad to know that his surgeon knew the lay out of his internal organs and good social attitudes would be no substitute. Somewhere along the line a student ought to have to get down to the chore of boning up on the hard core facts, even if it interfered with his private life.

It was sixteen hundred precisely when the group reached its last inspection point in the Cybernetics wing. The timetable said that Eisenberg would leave at sixteen thirty and so far it had been a routine exercise.

There was a barrier across the approach corridor and a couple of the resident campus security staff swung it away to let the party through.

Interest had flagged among the *hoi polloi* and only a dozen students, mainly women, were still around to see him go in.

The barrier was swung back behind a junior professor who had been at the tail end through the long afternoon and was finding his smile hard to keep going.

Cain drifted off to a lounge area on the floor, drew a coffee from a dispenser and lit his pipe. Leaned back on a reclining chair, he put his feet on a table and exercised personal choice.

Giving lateral thinking a chance, he let his mind drift over the known facts. Cybernetics had gone farther than was generally believed possible. Robot operators were a fact of life in many fields where routine handling was needed. Some of them were already very sophisticated items. These latest developments were one farther on but it was ridiculous to think that they could operate at an independent level.

The Eisenberg model must have been produced to make a convincing demonstration. Surrounded as he was by the top brass and his own colleagues, the man was in no danger.

Stringer's interest must have some other aim. But what that could be was not clear at this stage. There could be a number of interlocking motives. Human behaviour was never dead simple.

He finished his coffee and walked about. From the window he could see out to the parking lot. Eisenberg's official shuttle was moving from its pad to go to the main entrance for the pick up. Time was running out.

Two minutes later there was a surge of noise from the circulation space and he joined a knot of students to see the official party move past.

Eisenberg was still in the centre of the group. It was all over, a damp squib. Cain followed at a distance, watched him pose on the granite steps for another picture, wave and climb into his car.

A reporter followed up and got a couple of sentences for the record. The car rose into the metropolitan through way and picked up acceleration.

Crossing the lobby in a homegoing crush, Cain caught sight of an auburn ringlet swinging like a pendulum over a green and red check tabard and stepped behind her into the cage.

Dropping a hand on her shoulder he said, 'Well Mac, how's the fight with cholera today? Any chance of saving the city?'

'Oh it's you.'

'You keep saying that. The form of words is okay, but you haven't gotten the tone right. Try saying it with delighted rapture. Do you all the good in the world. Make as if your face was a round ring, radiating out like a radio signal in all directions, smile to the pips of your eyes. This physical mime of delight will work like yeast on your soul and produce the emotion itself. Tones up the skin, spreads subcutaneous fat, smoothes away wrinkles, keeps age at bay. Purse your lips as you say "you" and make your voice resonant.'

There was not a lot of room in the cage, but Christie Maclean found enough floor space to tap her foot while waiting for an opening. She had to concentrate to keep her mind on her lines and the question came out in a rush as they stopped at her floor.

'How did you know Cyril had cut his hand?'

He answered over the heads of the people moving with her onto the landing 'Simple deduction. He's just the sort to do that thing.'

86

Through the closing door she said, 'He's coming along tomorrow. You can get to know him better.'

Cain went through to his balcony and rattled the hanging chain.

She must have gone straight to the solar wall to look at her plant, because she was out at the second shake.

He said, 'Whose idea was that then? Don't you have any moral sense?'

'It's an open party. He's been on them before as it happens. When I said I was going he said he'd go along. I'll introduce you.'

'It's going to make it harder to get you alone in the bracken.'

'That's what I thought. But I'm sure you'll think of something. Don't build phantasies around this, but I didn't actually suggest it. He was just keen to come and, as I said, it's open to anyone interested in fresh air.'

She sniffed delicately at her geranium and closed the dialogue by moving out of vision through her hatch.

Art Delacroix was a puzzled man and looked frustrated as Cain held up his hand for silence. While Cain was shifting the pick up in a routine that was beginning to bore him to his root, he travelled about the apartment knocking out a rhythm on every resonant surface.

'How did you get on?'

'They had all those zombies in action. As far as I could remember the faces, they were set up as a student group. Other than the staff I could have been the only human being there about.'

'No trouble getting in?'

'Some. I wasn't popular. But I left it late and I suppose they didn't want a scene as he arrived.'

'Well then?'

'It's a biggish area as you saw. The inner door was open. I

guess we didn't check that too far. There could be other rooms. The official party split up. Eisenberg and one of his buddies went through and I tried to go in, but I was headed off. I couldn't have got in without open warfare and believe me with all those tin men pressing round it was no good.'

'So?'

'So he was out of sight for about five minutes, maybe less. Then he came back, spoke to the Director and they all moved off. He looked very pleased, said it was most impressive and Picton would be sure to get a sympathetic hearing when the estimates came up for review.'

'They could have switched him for the model?'

'You saw the model. Physically they could have. But it isn't on. I've been thinking about that. It wouldn't wash. There'd be a thousand things an android just wouldn't know however full the briefing tapes were. He'd fall down on some detail.'

'Theoretically I'd agree with that. But it's at least possible they have another angle that we haven't thought of. Before making that kind of venture, they'd think it out and objections that we see right away must have been considered.'

'But what's the point? Eisenberg's in the government and he's influential, but he's not right at the top. He couldn't swing any big useful decision on his own.'

'True. But it's a start. A big step to take. Also he walked right into it. He's the only one they could get on their own ground. Custom built for the exercise you might say. First thing to find out is whether the model is still in store. If its's gone, we'll be that much closer.'

'Where would that leave Eisenberg?'

'Nowhere good.'

'Tonight?'

'Tonight it is. Now that I know my way about, you don't have to come. In fact it might be better if you stayed home.'

'Now that I'm this far involved I'd like to see it through. I'll be there.'

Cain left it later. It was coming up to 0100 when they moved into the Cybernetics faculty and previous experience made him quicker with the locks.

There was no great change in the scene. The big work room could have been unused from the previous night. Delacroix stayed at the console and switched off when Cain was ready to slide away the inner hatch.

Cain's pencil beam flicked into the gap and he was a good half minute before he said, 'This I do not get. Switch on again.'

'Do you want a stampede?'

'Just switch on.'

The light revealed Delacroix with his laser ready to fire. He crossed the floor cautiously and stood beside Cain at the open hatch. Whatever he expected it was not this. The room was empty. Not only the Eisenberg model, but every other that had been in store was gone.

Cain said, 'Now that's surprising. They'd need a lot of transport to shift that circus. And where would they take them?'

He went inside and found a local console to flood the room with its own light.

Not revealed by the thin torch beam there were three ongoing sliding doors, easy to miss but not deliberately camouflaged. He tried them in turn. One was an engineer's store fitted with coded racks, everything from brass washers to skull frames built up of white plastic-sealed wire. The others were workshops for preliminary assembly and a couple of unfinished girls were leaned on support stands with a lipless grin.

Eisenberg could have been isolated in either for long enough to make a switch.

Delacroix rolled a folding screen from a wall cavity and made the action more plain.

It was nice to get it straight, but they were no nearer

the living proof. The man himself, if he was still drawing breath, had been evacuated to another part of the forest.

That required organization. Even if they went on their own feet. If Delacroix was right they were duplicates of regular members of the faculty. So where were the originals? Known to be out of the way for a period?

On the way back Cain said, 'Does your outfit have any students off on a trip at this time?'

'Some. In fact there's a flow in and out. Field study trips. They go look at industrial plants in the region. There's a hostel in the Preston area.'

'Have you been there?'

'Not yet. It's restricted to the last month of the course. Partly connected with the appointments service, so that people can see what kind of work's on offer.'

'Who arranges transport?'

'That I don't know. But it would have to be routed through the admin section. They'd pay the bill.'

'You go along home and make like two people occupying the premises. I'll be about a half hour.'

Cain let himself into the admin block from the courtyard where the black girl was still pitching in the dark. The main offices were above the entrance hall and he reckoned he was being optimistic. There were more doors than enough, with a variety of legends only making sense to the resident staff. Seen one at a time in the narrow beam of the torch they seemed endless.

He picked one labelled *Supply* and found himself in a long room packed with hardware. There was a fair flow of material into the Polytech and an automated accounts system to keep a neck lock on it.

At the end of the row he found a console devoted to daily transportation needs and rolled the record for the day's take. There were fifty-three items and listed for seventeen thirty hours was an allocation of two thirty-seater shuttles to Cybernetics with the admin director's authorisation.

The small print said they were bound for a point north of Blackburn City with an estimated round trip of a hundred kilometres. The address given was Field Study Centre Three, Precinct Nine.

On the way out he noticed *Student Records* on another door and thought it might as well be his night for information.

Each faculty had its console and he sat at the Cybernetics desk and played through the nominal roll. Faces flipped by on the scanner with condensed biographical detail on a running strip.

Delacroix grinned amiably at him and slipped by. It was difficult to tell whether he was recognizing others or not until he came to the girl. She had gone past before he could stop the flow and he had to backtrack. Then there was no doubt. It was the one all right. Samantha Jones. No parents living. Something of a drifter having tried several jobs. Highly rated on intelligence and came to Picton from Newport City.

So she was a natural for any experiment. No visiting relative was going to appear with a fruit cake and ask her what she was doing with a duralumin spine.

Cain went through the rest. He positively identified another four as being part of the zombie party. All without close ties. Either they had been selected on that basis from the roll or had even been admitted in the first place because they fitted the bill.

It was something the department ought to know. That and his theory about Eisenberg.

Delacroix called through the connecting hatch as soon as he was in his room.

'Bob?'

'Here present. Hold it. I'll come through.'

Delacroix had his flask at his elbow and was sitting at his desk with the laser handy. 'I've had a visitor in here.

91

Nothing gone, but things have been moved. I have this photographic memory for where I put things and everything's just that bit different.'

'I guess they're puzzled. Hang on, I'll be back.'

Cain dragged out his cabin trunk. The visitor had looked at it for a sure thing. The aerial system had been wrecked. He went for his razor. That too was strictly a salvage job. The home gas chamber kit had disappeared.

He rejoined Delacroix and took a long pull from the offered flask. He said, 'This is one hell of a college. It makes you despair of higher education. Tomorrow will be very interesting. Just so we have the pleasure of taking part in it, we should get out of here tonight. Pack your toothbrush and those jazzy pyjamas and we'll take a room in town. To get the best out of the scenery, we need to be all fresh and rested up.'

'That suits me. I don't fancy another sentry go.'

The party that gathered on the porch was smaller than Cain expected. Stringer was there with a check board ticking off arrivals in baggy shorts, long knitted socks and heavy lace boots.

Brigitta Ross had frayed suede pants, a bolero with maximum gusset interest and thick soled sneakers. A nondescript couple holding hands stood at one side studying a folding map. Cain remembered he had seen them at the back of the Vorticist meeting.

He went to Brigitta and introduced Delacroix. 'It's a pity you didn't bring your actualiser, he'd have fixed it for you in no time at all. He has a fantastic knack.'

'I can imagine.'

Speaking up for himself, the expert said, 'Not to worry. It's more a domestic talent. I can show you when we get back.'

'That's all right. I guess it can take its chance in the inscrutable future.'

92

'If we meet a goat on this mountain you're going to need a steady nerve.'

Cain left them and went to the host. 'Where are they all then? There was a long list.'

'Only two more from here. A medico and a man from outside called Donovan. The main party join at Grasmere. They're at a Field Study Centre and they'll leave from there.'

The two arrived at the same time, Donovan from the street and Christie Maclean from the lobby.

Cain went to meet her. Donovan said 'Hi' and went to talk to Stringer.

In the morning light it was as ordinary and casual as it could get. Cain had a feeling that he was the only one out of step and had gotten it all wrong. He had been too long in the business and was suffering from illusion.

She was looking very practical and trim in a green hunting tartan with a long sleeved button through cyclamen shirt and carrying a small rucksack by the straps.

He said, 'Shouldn't you have a little knife in your stocking to slice your salami?'

Stringer called out, 'That's it. We can get away. Nothing like an early start.' He led off with Donovan and they climbed into a ten seater shuttle, which had parked on the apron below the steps.

The sense of discontinuity grew on Cain. Delacroix took Brigitta Ross to the rumble and from her giggle seemed to have found a satisfactory fill in for his knack. The two club members were on a closed communication loop. Donovan and Stringer, an unlikely pair, were in a huddle over a guide book on the squab behind the pilot.

Christie Maclean watched the town give way to the green belt and said, 'What's got into you then? That's the longest time you've been silent in our short acquantance. Are you still mad about Cyril coming along?'

'No. Just another side of my nature. Reflective. Deep if you like. I was thinking about the city. From here, looking down at people moving around, it wouldn't matter whether they were people or not. They could be androids.'

'Who wouldn't it matter to?'

'To the observer.'

'What kind of idea is that? It would matter to them— supposing, which I don't, that they would know about it.'

'You know android development has gone a long way. What's so special about a biological brain that makes it better than a mechanical one?'

'Is that a serious question?'

'Take it that way.'

She swivelled on the seat to face him and judge for herself.

With a memory of Samantha Jones he tried to see her as an android figure. Maybe the art department could copy the hair and the eyes with their spectacular white cornea. Where was the core of the difference that made her human?

Even the voice had a measureable wave structure, timbre, harmonics, that could be analysed by a computer and simulated by a man-made structure.

She said slowly, 'It's the mind-body relationship that makes the difference. Sure they can build a brain that can gather information and make decisions on it. But a biological system has a special rhythm. It's born, it grows and it dies. It has to live with itself in the framework of that knowledge.'

'That could be built into an android.'

'But it wouldn't *care*.'

'It could have a self regarding capability built in and a group survival factor for that matter. Every situation can be broken down into component parts that can be recognized and given a value.'

'I'm not thinking just of self sacrifice for the good of the android group. Insects do that anyway without having human values. It's the whole growth pattern. Right from pre-natal time. Dependence, affection, a long period of growth with changing needs, relating to the biological world because you're part of it. Androids are a tool like a hand axe, they don't have an existence outside any use we might have for them.'

Christie Maclean's dark brown eyes were very serious. Seen close from half a metre range, they were remarkable examples of evolution in their own right and a living proof that there was more to a human argument than the spoken text.

An android could have said it with the right intonation, but the eyes transmitted a carrier wave for emotion and personal conviction. She believed it and wanted him to believe it.

'I hope you're right. Strictly on those terms I'd say you *were* right. But we don't know what an android would be like after fifty years of moving about and absorbing experience. After a point it could take off and turn into something unexpected. A human being is only the sum of its personal history. Nothing comes out of the biological computer that hasn't gone in at some point. A few people get a new slant on an old idea once in a way.'

Brigitta Ross had come forward from the rumble in a prudent bid to keep her options open for a few more kilometres and leaned over the seat between them breathing out heady fumes of rye. She was only on circuit for the last sentence but she agreed with it. 'That's your friend. A thumb nail sketch.'

Cain said, 'We were talking about androids and Christie has it that a human operator has the edge all the time.'

'I don't think I know any androids, but from observation at the bar I'd say it would be a close run thing. There's a lot of very rigid behaviour pattern from the naked ape. Like he was programmed by a standard blue tape. Now an android would be all for intellectual chat. How much water flows through the Morecambe Barrage in thirty three seconds and keen items like that. Make a

95

girl feel wanted for herself. Maybe Christie's right. Yes on mature judgement I'd go along with her. You're outvoted two to one.'

A sharp whip crack made a period. Delacroix had leaned out of his seat and scored a flat handed bull's eye on the taut chamois-covered can angled his way.

He said, 'For godsake Brigitta come and sit down. Bending over like that you make me think I'm on safari stalking some antelope.'

It was a telling point and she gave them a significant look. 'You see what I mean?'

The shuttle had climbed into the subsonic inter city freeway and was streaking over undulating moorland at its maximum cruising rate of six hundred kilometres in the hour. Then it was planing down, skirting Keswick City on a by pass and dropping to the local zone connector way to thread the valleys.

When it sighed to a halt on the apron of the Tourist and Climbing Centre Hotel, the other party was already assembled.

First in view was Samantha Jones in an Arran knit sweater and a white bobble hat. Well equipped for an orphan, she had an expensive looking camera on a shoulder strap and binoculars on a thong around her neck.

Stringer said, 'Leave your packs here. They'll be taken on and left where we stop for lunch.'

CHAPTER SIX

By noon the field was well strung out with Donovan up ahead with Stringer and a small knot of eager beavers.

Delacroix and his antelope were way back in the column. Cain and Christie Maclean topped a steep rise and found a long calm view of rounded hills shading into blue distance and a tongue of lake pushing out round a spur three or four hundred metres below.

She said, between deep breaths, 'I'm glad I came. This is lovely. Trite though it sounds in the guide book this is a refreshment to the spirit.'

'A handsome admission. As time goes by you will come to say "He knows best. I will follow his advice in every particular." That's a human judgement. In your view an android wouldn't react with an aesthetic judgement?'

'Why should it? There wouldn't be any practical value. Why would it make a trip like this anyway?'

'It would only risk rusting a cog by sitting on damp grass?'

'Right.'

Samantha Jones's bobble hat topped the rise and she came into full view, walking with an easy tireless swing.

Cain said suddenly, 'Let's ask one.'

'What do you mean?'

But he had already moved off and planted himself in the track.

Samantha had the choice of walking into him or

passing the time of day. She hove to with a non-committal smile.

Cain said, 'How does it go Samatha? We'd like your opinion on the view.'

Voice unaffected by the steep climb, she said, 'That's easy. It's beautiful. In the mountains, you feel free. It puts the city in perspective.'

'That's a thick sweater for a mild day and a stiff climb, but you don't look as though your motor was over-heating.'

'I'm used to it. What is this anyway?'

'Just a medical check point to see that you can go the distance. Roll up your jumper and my medical friend will listen to your heart beat.'

'Suppose I say no?'—she was looking warily around for support, but there was nobody in sight.

Cain's laser appeared in his hand, 'I might just decide to make some gaps in your circuit.'

Christie Maclean said sharply 'Have you gone out of your head? Let her pass.'

Samantha's hands went to the hem of her jersey then came out straight in a double grab for the gun. It was very smooth and quick and the eyes had given nothing away.

Cain moved as fast, dropped the laser and was down on one knee bringing her over his head. He was astride her with Christie Maclean's fists pounding on his back, feeling a surge of power from the prone figure that he knew he could not hold. Then he had her hat pulled over her eyes and she went limp.

Christie Maclean's voice cut in again. She had gathered up the laser and sounded all set to use it. 'You're a maniac. Let her go.'

Cain shoved away the sweater and stood up.

'Look for yourself.'

'It's a trick. You want to get your gun back.'

'I'll go and stand over there.'

From three metres off, he watched Christie Maclean

kneel beside the girl keeping the laser lined up on his chest.

Then she had put it down on the turf and was saying, 'Oh no. I can't believe it. It's obscene.'

Cain joined her. Put his gun back in its clip and helped her to her feet. Arm round her shoulders, he said soberly, 'It's a lot to take in at one go.'

He turned her slowly towards him.

'What are you going to do?'

'Nothing as of now.'

Eyes threaded on a double string there was another argument going on at a different level. For the first time in years he was wholly sidetracked, seeing another human being as a person with a point of view and small pale areas beside her nose that looked vulnerable and bare of artifice.

A small scuff of movement from behind her had him pushing her roughly out of line and a heavy camera swung by its strap like a ball and chain beat down through the gap between them.

Samantha had drawn herself quietly to her feet and was making a policy statement. The follow through put her a little off balance, but she recovered, threw down the strap; wheeled away and went at a run over the brow of the hill.

Christie Maclean said 'Did you see her face? It meant nothing at all. She was smiling. It wouldn't have mattered if she'd killed us.'

'That's a very odd thing.'

'Odd. You call it *odd*? It's diabolical.'

'Not that. I'd got the idea that the on/off switch for these monkeys was photo-electric. She went limp when I covered her eyes. But some other mechanism came in to get her restarted. That looks like remote control. Monitored from somewhere. Now that's something new.'

'Are you saying that you knew all about it? You were taking a chance.'

99

'Think back. Do you remember this girl Samantha Jones coming through your medicentre?'

'I'd notice that. They strip off.'

'The real Samantha Jones.'

'A lot go through at the beginning of the session. All girls look alike to me.'

'That's a good speech. It shows your interest's in the right place.'

'There'd be a record. Anyway I can say she looked vaguely familiar. You mean this one's a copy of a registered student? What about the original? Where does she fit into it?'

'That's the sixty-four thousand dollar question.'

What will she do now?'

'That's a subsidiary question, but also important. Let's take a look. Up the hillside for a bird's eye view.'

They were fifteen minutes climbing the spur. Fifty metres of scree, some rough slopes and ten metres vertical travel up a crag face before they could see ahead.

Samantha, a diminished figure, was loping along and within a hundred metres of the main body. It was just possible to make out Stringer's fuzzy head with Donovan still beside him.

There was a general halt and heads turned to show the pale oval of faces as they waited for her to catch up.

She went straight to Stringer.

Over the other side of the hill there was a group of six together and then two farther back. Too far to reach with any warning. Delacroix and Brigitta had trailed to the end of the column. The six had stopped and were looking forward as though they too were listening to the tale of assault.

Stringer was talking to his group like a general giving a briefing. Then he and Donovan were left alone with the rest streaming back at a jog trot. The six moved off at the same time. There was no doubt it was a pincer movement. The word had gone out to bring in the foiled rapist.

Christie Maclean said, 'They believe her. She's told some tale and they think you attacked her.'

'That's not the half of it. If I'm right they're all the same outfit.'

'Androids? How could they get away with that? Surely there'd have been some leak before now.'

'As I see it the operation is moving into a new phase. This could be the first mass exercise.'

Down below, the two parties had made contact. Samantha herself was pointing dramatically to the spot and holding out her battered camera for ocular proof. There was a scatter round. It was plain that the quarry could not have gone down and gotten out of vision in the time. So the answer was up. They spread out like a line of beaters, five metres apart and began to climb the hill at the same steady jog trot.

Different they might be in size and shape, but they were uniform in action, legs pounding in time like so many pistons. Cain had a sudden vision of a company of them in field grey with carbines at the high port sweeping towards a strong point. It only needed a production line and Vort or whoever was at the centre could build himself an unstoppable army corps.

They would be the perfect military type. Intelligent, obedient, expendable, without personal fear.

They were in the scree, sliding a little but pressing on. It was time to go. He pulled Christie Maclean to her feet and they ran hand in hand over a grass covered plateau with a gentle rise to a bare outcrop with a steep scramble face.

Half way up Cain stopped. Heads were breaking the sky line like so many round buildings. Face flushed with effort, chest heaving prettily in her cyclamen shirt, Christie Maclean said, 'It's no good, Bob. This won't stop them.'

The line had grown tall again. There was a signal

forward and they were running, covering the ground at twice the speed of any human climber.

Cain got them moving, covering fifteen metres of a near vertical pitch without a check.

'All right, Chris?'

'It has to be. Keep moving.'

The first androids had reached the base of the crag. Wiping sweat out of his eyes, Cain saw an economical division of forces. Some went loping off on either flank for a long detour, half a dozen including Samantha Jones started in on the climb.

There was ten metres to go to an overhang and they had to traverse for a cleft and a steep winding ascent over loose rock.

Cain lay flat and shoved his head and shoulders over the drop.

Except that they had no fatigue problem the androids had no advantage. They were taking it slowly, picking hand holds as though they were running every choice through a computer.

Samantha was leading the field and almost directly below. He picked out a small craggy boulder and dropped it on her head.

It hit sure and true and she was half a minute struggling to keep from following it into free fall. But her grip held. The same was not true of her hair. Together with her bobble hat a blonde wig was following the rock. The fixed smile was still there, but under a shiny pink dome it had no element of friendship in it.

Christie Maclean had already begun a stumbling jog trot away from the edge.

They had the top to themselves. It could have been empty from the time when Stone Age man roamed around picking likely flints for a hand axe. The sky was clear, the hills were bare and silent. It was a good day for a walk at that.

Cain reckoned bitterly that if he'd been trying to get

the girl alone, it would have been full of jolly parties photographing each other beside a sheep.

They were a hundred metres ahead before the first androids heaved themselves over the lip and made another fifty while the line formed. Individuals would have run on. This posse was under discipline. But it would pay off. There would be no dodging through a gap in the column.

The slope was deceptive, steeper for fifty metres and then levelling off with coarser tufted grass and they were sinking in soft ground.

Christie Maclean panted, 'Marsh. We'll have to go back.'

'Keep going.'

They were sinking ankle deep, slowed to a walk, trying to pick a way. Cain forged ahead, programmed to keep moving, pulling her by main force. Any minute he expected to see the flanking force appear to box them in.

Pulled sideways she was free to look back and gave him a sitrep. 'It's all right. They've stuck in it. Look.'

It was true. Carrying more weight, the androids were finding the going tough. They appeard to have shortened by half a metre. Sunk to the calves, they were out of rhythm, forced to go on, but short on technique for a situation outside experience.

Cain reached harder ground and heaved the girl after him. She had lost a shoe and stopped long enough to pull off the other.

He used the time to drop on one knee, cradle his laser on his forearm and make a marksman's job of dropping a fine bisecting line from forehead to navel on the centre man of the operation. He could see the mark he made, a thin furrow that was opened farther by the effort the man was making but it did not stop him. Whatever damage was done to the higher centre, the mechanical drive was untouched. He came right on, heaving one leg after the other out of the bog.

They went on. Veering right with the logic of the

ground, Cain trying to visualise the run of the minor surface roads in the area.

The ground was rising slightly again and they made the crest of it. Below was a short steep slide to a dry stone wall and a narrow ribbon of track. A three wheeled surface scooter was parked on the grass and two figures with rucksacks and climbing gear were working up the facing slope.

Cain raced for the scooter. The console was sealed by a slide cover locked in place. He burned out the lock with a broad set laser beam and was busy sorting through an unfamiliar layout of switchgear against the mind bending clamor of an anti-thief siren, when Christie Maclean arrived. At the same time, he saw androids spilling from cover left and right on the road.

He was in the saddle with the girl on the pillion, shoving down the pin for maximum thrust.

She grabbed for his waist by simple reflex and hung on as the scooter bucked away with Cain spinning the wheel for a sliding turn.

He went down the lane in a howl of acceleration, learning control the hard way in a series of swerves that took them from edge to edge of the narrow tarmac.

The androids tried. Untroubled by the personal survival kick, they lined up shoulder to shoulder across the way.

Cain held on, then made a last minute change, slewed along the front of the phalanx to the grass slope, took it at a crazy angle and came down again to fight for control over the next hundred metres.

Christie Maclean, ringlet flying back like a red gold pennant in the morning sun was shouting in his ear to beat the demented wail of the siren, 'You did it. You did it.'

The road was twisting like a gut, dropping between a pair of walls that made it strictly single lane. A small party of regular tourists with knobbly sticks flung themselves left and right and they were through to a ragged volley of shouts.

Cain drove half a kilometre and pulled in on a stony lay-by beside a bridge. He located the siren in a sealed unit below the chassis and blasted it with his laser until it shut off with a death rattle.

The silence was unexpected and Christie Maclean's voice was over loud for it when she said, 'The owner isn't going to like that.'

'If he's any sense he'll have it insured.'

'Not for riot and civil disorder.'

'What are you on about? You stand there in your bare feet with your shirt tail out rabbitting on about law and order. Don't you realize you're lucky to be taken out on a nature trail? Get back on your perch and we'll go down to the village and see what we can find.'

With the pressure off there was time to take in the full spectrum. There was some heat in the sun, clouds were very white and the shape of the hills was satisfying to the mind.

Still dubious about pillion mechanics, Christie Maclean kept a close bear hug round his waist and there was a comfortable pneumatic pressure against his back. Cain began to sing 'Shenandoah', aware that it was out of context, but reckoning that it had an appropriate folksy ambience.

It got a giggle and a warm pressure against the back of his neck that sent them in a swerve.

'Was that a vote of confidence?'

'Provisional.'

'Provisional on what?'

'I don't know. Don't analyse a gesture too closely.'

'We psychologists like to know where we are. Get after a motive like a hunting pack.'

'Keep your eyes on the road or your enquiring mind is going to have to find another body.'

They rounded a bluff and were on top of a small cluster of

stone buildings. There was a triangular green with a sign post on a stone plinth, a bridge, an inn, a row of grey stone cottages and a long, low general purpose store with a pillared frontage like an updated cloister.

There was also a parking lot floored with loose granite chips. Cain ran the scooter between a long distance shuttle and a farm tractor and killed the motor. He was out of the saddle before she could move and lifted her off her seat.

When he put her down on the grass verge she said, 'I was wondering about walking on that.But I should have realized, you think of everything.'

'Some things more than others, but taken in the broadest sense you could be right.'

'And modest with it. Did you know it was going to turn out like this when you invited me along?'

'No.'

'Can I believe that?'

'Virtue mine honour.'

'That should be my line.'

'In these troubled times who knows where they stand? Let's see what they have in the village store.'

There was a scatter of visitors turning over souvenirs at a long counter in the middle. Either end had a serving area, one for prepacked grocery items, the other with a wide range from camping gear to snowflake tights.

Christie Maclean found a pair of rope soled sandals and said, 'My credit card's in my pack. What do we use for money?'

'My pleasure. Is there anything else you'd like? They do some gnomes in a snow scene with "We are Seven" in Gothic script. Or a scarf with acrobatic Hindu figures and Wordsworth's cottage.'

'Not a thing.'

'You're a hard girl to please.'

The proprietor, a tall oldster in a forage cap and a turtle neck sweater with a weather beaten face and a stoop took the card and fed it into his computer.

Cain said, 'Does Professor Vort ever come in here?'

There was no answer until the machine had rung up acceptance of the deal and signalled Cain's national credit rating. It seemed to reassure the trader.

'Do you know him?'

'By repute. I'm at the college where he used to teach. I heard he'd retired into these parts to contemplate and creep towards death.'

'He's a queer one.'

'You do see him then?'

'Not for a long time. Must be a year or eighteen months maybe since he was in here. They all keep themselves to themselves.'

'They?'

'There's a big staff up there,'—he jerked a gaunt thumb at the road winding off up the valley. 'It ought to be good for trade in the dead season when the hikers stop coming. But it isn't. I guess they have everything sent along from Keswick City. Occasionally a few get down to the pub. They don't stay long and don't mix with the locals. There's two local men at the lodge. Two brothers. Always thought to be queer round here. Still everybody has a right to go his own way. I like to please myself, so I can't grumble,'

'Where is this place of his, then?'

'You won't get in if you were thinking of paying a call. Nobody gets past the lodge without a personal invitation. Since the road was closed to through traffic it isn't much used except by walkers who go over the top by Stonethwaite Fell into the next valley. It's not half a kilometre along. On the left. There's a small gill with a beck running through. Sealed off except for one entrance at the lodge. Some say it used to be a gunpowder plant centuries back. They have a hydro electric plant.'

'It sounds as though you've been inside at least.'

'I've lived here man and boy for seventy-five years. When I was a youngster we used to go in there for a swim, there are mill ponds to gather a head of water. It's got a funny atmosphere though. We'd never go except in a party. Big stone grinding wheels lying about and water falling every whichway. Cold too as I recall. Freeze the balls off of a brass monkey, even on a hot day. If the young lady will pardon the expression.'

'That's all right, she's a medic. Used to fearless, scientific truth.'

There was a pause. The old man looked up the valley, caught on a memory loop. Christie Maclean finished fastening her sandals. Cain filled his pipe and when it was lit asked another question.

'It's been built up since those days?'

'There's about a hectare of near level ground. Some buildings were on it, all shuttered up. About twenty years back there was a lot of activity. The work was done by a firm in Preston. Nobody local made anything out of it. It went on for a couple of years give or take a month or two. Transporters coming and going all the time. Must have cost a packet. Then it all quietened down. But they get plenty of visitors. By air mostly. Drop right into the centre.'

'Well thanks a lot. That's very interesting. Can we get a meal around here?'

'At *The Oak*. Expensive but very good.'

Settled in a low raftered dining room with much hanging copperware Cain dabbed a fleck of froth off his beard and sniffed at his ragout. If the affidavit was to be believed there was real local meat in it.

Christie Maclean said, 'I've asked myself and come up with the answer that for the first time today I'm beginning to like this place.'

'I like a girl who likes her food.'

'Not just the food. It's the atmosphere. Even the tourist gimmicry can't kill it. It's soaked into the walls. This is an enclave where the pace is right. I'd like to be here in the winter.'

'With a sheep carcase in the rafters and beer ferment-ing with a low gurgle.'

'Don't laugh at me.'

'I'm not laughing. You have a point. But there's an outfit over the way like a Trojan Horse. Vort's androids wouldn't want the simple life. They'd trade a pint of ale for a pint of oil any day of the week. And you can't make high grade oil in an old bucket.'

'I'm sorry you mentioned that, but since you have, what do you intend to do?'

'First things first. I've just seen Phyllis there take a slice of blueberry pie to the corner table. Blueberry pie and cream and a cup of Gaelic coffee. That restores the initiative to the human faction. That Samantha now would get it all over her cogs and wouldn't enjoy it.'

He signalled for service and there was a digestive pause. Christie Maclean tackled her pie with neat surgical gestures.

Mouth pleasantly purple, she took up the argument, 'But that's not much of an edge for the human mind. I go for blueberry pie with the next, but you can't base a whole philosophy on it.'

'You're changing your ground. You were the one rooting for man's special place.'

'That was when I didn't believe it could be challenged. Now I want some good collaterals.'

'From where I sit, there's the best. You look gorgeous. Now an android wouldn't notice that. Or if he did, it wouldn't do anything for him. Now it makes me feel very cheerful and optimistic.'

'That's the liquor.'

'No cynicism, Mac. Eros makes the whole world tick.'

'That's a dodgy basis for progress.'

'It all depends in which direction you are aiming to go.'

'Shouldn't we be getting out of here? It's a bit close to the line of march. As I remember the route, they were to come back this way for the pick up at eighteen hundred.'

'You have a point. But I'd like to look at Vort's place.'
Pie had not dulled her wits.
'Do you think there's a connection?'
'There's a connection.'
'But the man said you couldn't get in.'
'Maybe nobody has tried too hard.'
'When do we start then?'
'We don't. You stay here and keep out of sight. I'll be back within the hour.'

She was ready to argue about it. Eyes across the table were signalling mutiny and a stand for women's rights under the constitution.

But what she saw sold the pass at a level where verbalizing had no place. She looked away out of the window, presenting him with a smoothly satisfying jaw line. Her voice only carried across the table when she said, 'Very well. Have it your own way. Where do I hide? In the powder room?'

'Not a bad choice. Samantha and company won't be needing to use it. Write picture cards to your friends. Female friends. I wouldn't want you encouraging followers. Look at your watch every few minutes and think, "He will soon be with me again". But do not confuse your own heartbeats with the approaching footsteps of your lover.'

'Why not?'

'God knows. But it must have happened occasionally or there wouldn't be the ancient warning.'

'If it goes dark, I'll light a lamp in the window.'

'A wise move in the situation. See you then.'

He reached the door before she could move and she had to run to catch him on the forecourt.

'Wait.'

'What is it?'

'I got a shivery feeling. Like a premonition. Take care.'

'I won't go swimming in his pool for a sure thing.'

'Goodbye then.'

'A bientot.'

Cain passed the entrance to Vort's place in six minutes of brisk walking. He had followed a high wall of grey stone blocks topped by an out curving system of concrete fence posts which carried a fine wire mesh. Behind them was a thick copse planted with the precision of a forestry commission lot. Staggered in depth, they were an effective screen for any building work that lay beyond.

The entrance itself had been developed to give clear vision along either flank. There was an old lodge on the right, a new building on the left in the same architectural style to satisfy the planners and a connecting structure overhead so that all traffic was funnelled through a short tunnel.

Flooring under the arch was loose close-set rods, running from edge to edge. Nothing could pass without making a rattle. Though ten to one that was the least sophisticated item of checking equipment.

A square set man in grey, belted coveralls and a forage cap with a Phoenix badge came out of a narrow door and watched him go by.

Cain slowed, turned around and went back. The man had stayed still watching him.

He made no move as Cain went right up to him.

'What place is this? It doesn't figure on the map.'

'Private property, Mister. There'd be no call to show it.'

'I thought this was all open walking country.'

'Not this part. Like I said it's private property.'

'Who lives here then?'

'It's a Research Institute. Private outfit.'

'Very private by the look of it.'

'There's no law against that. With all the people swarmin' around here in the summer, you need a wall. If everybody who had a mind to do it cut themself a walking stick, there'd not be a tree left standin'.'

'What research do they do in there?'

'Look, mister. I just look out for this gate and mind my own business.'

Without turning his head he raised his voice and called out, 'Alf, I've got a right one for askin' questions.'

He was joined by another lodge keeper in the same uniform, who must have been handy just inside the door. This one was taller with a long grey face and had a riot stick hanging from his belt.

'What's the matter?'

'This fella with the face hair is askin' what goes on inside.'

'What does he want to know for?'

Cain broke into the vaudeville act before the punch line, 'Just forget it. Pretend I never asked. I'll get on my way.'

They were standing together watching him out of sight as he turned a bend a hundred metres up the road.'

There was still the high wall on his left and it ran on for another hundred metres, then it turned smartly away from the road, ran across a paddock, crossed the beck which ran through under an arch and butted into the side of a steep craggy slope.

He climbed a five barred gate into the paddock and followed the wall to the side of the beck. For ten metres the river bed had been cleared, deepened and lined with slabs of green slate. Water was running like a smooth glass sheet with a depth of between two and three metres. At its centre the arch in the wall gave three metres head room to allow for flood conditions in heavy rain. A plaque in red said 'Keep Out. Electronic debris control.'

On the face of it, a swimmer could float himself through on the current with no trouble at all. But it couldn't be that simple. With all the precautions else-where, they wouldn't leave such an obvious entry point unguarded.

He went along the bank to the end of the engineered

section, took off his shoes and waded into the shallows calf deep. It was wholly cold.

Bent double he could see through the arch. There was greater thickness than could be expected from a simple wall. Maybe three metres of smooth stonework. At the far end there was a tooth edge as though a grille had been hauled up and could be dropped to close it off.

Cain searched around, found a loose fence post and heaved it out. Using his laser, he cut off some lengths of galvanized wire, gathered brushwood and a couple of sticks and bound the lot together in the rough shape of a scarecrow.

Wading out again he launched the mockup in mid stream and got down to water level to watch it through.

The surface current was slow and it took its time, getting itself into a slow lateral spin. Cain could feel his hands and feet going numb. Through the arch he could see a small quadrant of sky and the slaty wall of the ravine where the course of the beck took a turn towards the road.

His log man reached the arch, idled round in another turn and slipped underneath. There was a brief surge of light, with the inside of the tunnel made brilliantly plain. The far end had closed itself off and a bronze coloured grid had dropped in place.

The water inside was boiling white. The log was a dark stain and then it was gone.

The grid slowly retracted, the disturbed water ran clear. He could have imagined the whole sequence.

He collected his shoes and socks, crossed the stream, sat on a rock to put them on and began to climb the hill.

It was tough going and he got the impression that sections of the slope had been worked over to discourage the casual walker. Certainly the pitch above the wall itself had been smoothed out so that only a roped team could get close.

At the top the area overlooking the ravine was enclosed

by a four metre fence on concrete pylons with every other strand running through massive insulation sleeves. Beyond it was a collection of long sheds in a state of decay with moss growing on their slate roofs. Heaps of green slate were scattered about. It had been the surface installation of a quarry.

He followed the fence and at one point where it ran close to the lip, he could look down into the quarry itself, a vast sombre hole with a small still lake of rust streaked water, in the depths.

Completing the circuit, he came out to a narrow surface road and judged that it would take him down to the village. His watch told him he had already taken an hour.

Time to go. Nothing gained except an estimate of how difficult the mission was.

Going down the hill he passed a couple of elderly women with identical short-cropped grey hair, dressed in mountaineering kit with heavy boots and thick brown stockings. They were followed by a fat, discontented spaniel which was dragging its feet and looked as though it had gotten sick to the stomach with weekend excursions.

They gave him a hard look, clearly writing him off as a non-serious visitor. Cain waved a cheerful hand as he went by saying 'Good afternoon. A fine day for it.'

The one nearest to him said sharply to the dog, 'Come along Bounty,' as though she was aiming to keep it safe from fraternization.

It gave him a look from liquid brown eyes that said as plain as words 'Don't blame me. It's my meal ticket.'

There was more activity in the village. Walkers who had made it a pick up point had gathered after the day's march.

From half way down the hill he could see a dozen or more sitting around the stone cross with long drinks they had carried out of *The Oak*.

There was a bridge over the beck and just before he

reached it, he crossed an access road that led to the quarry.

It was closed by massive iron gates and the way beyond was steep and narrow curving away through a deep cutting.

A faded notice said, *Mountain Manufacture and Mining Co.* Below it was another, more recent, with *Private Land Keep Out.*

He stopped again on the bridge and looked up the beck towards Vort's empire. Trees came down to the beckside in a close copse. Fifty metres along,the wall completed its circuit and dovetailed into the side of the Mining Company's property.

Very likely at this point in time Vort had acquired the quarry land to complete the fourth side of his valley. It was was all very tightly wound up.

The store was doing brisk business with a good crowd milling about shoving souvenirs into rucksacks.

He went into *The Oak* and checked out the small lounge. She was not there. He crossed to the store and walked round the counters. No dice.

Back at the inn, he found the waitress who had served the meal and said, 'Have you seen the girl who who was with me?'

'She left.'

'When was this?'

'Fifteen, twenty minutes back.'

'Did you see where she went?'

'Met a friend. Tall handsome guy. Talked for a time. Then they left.'

'Did you see which way?'

'We were just getting busy so I didn't notice.'

'Well thanks.'

'My pleasure. There was another girl with them by the way. Blonde type. I heard him call her Samantha. Wearing a see through shirt. Should be listed as unfair trading practice.'

CHAPTER SEVEN

Cain left *The Oak* with a bitter sense that he had been too clever by half. Running solo was one thing and the department expected it, but getting a bystander caught up in the web was another. He ought to have played it alone. Bringing Christie Maclean had been a self indulgence which would be hard to live with.

He checked the time. Nearly two hours before the party gathered at the Tourist and Climbing Centre. He could make it easy, going straight over the fell into the next valley.

If she was in Vort's block house, no frontal approach would spring her. He had no right to try. The information so far ought to go to Fraser.

A group had gathered in the parking lot and a public safety shuttle with the Federal Environment blazon on its coachwork was drawn up on the road.

It looked as though the owner had caught up with his scooter and was complaining to the law enforcement branch.

He detoured, keeping out of sight below the brow of the hill and struck off up a winding track.

He had it to himself and there was all the time in the world to consider the angles. First in line was the certainty that he should have told her more about Donovan. She could have been on guard.

Then he stopped still and looked at a brand new concept. It was one that ought to have come up before and it was a measure of the girl's unique charm that it hadn't.

The bystander report made no mention of argument. There had been no attempt to leave a message. She could be in on the act. Possibly not in Stringer's organization, though she had been on these rural junkets in the past. But possibly in Donovan's scheme of reference. She was well placed to be an agent. The hypo had been routed through the medi centre. Maybe he was wasting his sympathy.

He cracked off again and made the top of the rise in a sustained burst of effort that brought him out in a sweat.

Whichever way it was, there was only one line to take. He had to go along with the situation as it was presented. If they were having a quiet belly laugh, that was okay.

Some of the heat had gone out of the day and he went down the reverse slope running for a hundred metres, then walking, running again, hitting a rhythm that emptied his mind.

He was early at the RV. The shuttle was there, but only two of the outgoing party. The two nondescript Vorticists had gotten back to base and were drinking lager beer on the porch of the hotel.

Cain joined them and they moved closer together giving him a nod as though strings had been pulled in unison.

Cain went through collected a beer and joined them. 'Did you have a good day?'

The man said, 'Couldn't be better. It's nice at this time of the year. Not so crowded.'

'I didn't see you on the line of march.'

'We know it pretty well. Been often. We usually strike out on our own route.'

'You missed the excitement then?'

'What excitement?'

'Some of the party got involved with a stolen scooter.'

'No we didn't see anything of that.'

He gave it up and leaned on a rail. A group of half a dozen were coming into the village, talking and laughing together. They clattered up the steps to the porch and went inside to the bar.

They were all members of the group that had come on from the study centre and had been part of the android posse.

He followed them in, watched them order and saw the leading hand, a tall sallow man in his early twenties sink a pint of ale in a slow wager-winning swallow.

It got a big hand and there was no gripe from the machinery. They were all at it.

Cain said, 'A good day?' and collected an incurious set of eyes. Not unfriendly but negative. No recognition. If they had chased him through a bog they had forgotten all about it.

But then the drinking was no big problem. With all the rest of the sophisticated gear it would be simple to put in a disposal sack. Very necessary in fact for the Eisenberg *doppelganger*. That one would have official banquets to attend and even an eccentric would not be excused for slipping his *Sole Meuniere* into his brief case.

One of the girls, a friendly plump type with an engaging moustache of white froth said 'It was lovely, we went right over the top. How far did you get?'

'Did you see anything of a girl with auburn hair and a green kilt as you came in?'

'The medico? Christie something. I know who you mean. But no. I guess not. Stringer will know where she is. He always gets in last whipping in the stragglers.'

'You've been out and about all day then in the wind and the sun?'

'Surely, what else?'

Cain gave it up and went on the porch to look out for Stringer. The girl had spoken truth, he came in at the tail end with a group singing 'Green Grow the Rushes O'.

Samantha Jones was walking beside him putting in a contralto descant.

There was a general move toward the shuttle and Stringer with Samantha Jones beside him checked off his flock on his tally stick.

Cain joined them at the hatch. It was even true about the girl's shirt. Anybody sticking a screwdriver in her symmetrical navel would get a well modulated scream and a slapped wrist. She was all woman and giggly with it.

Cain leaned on the panel and spoke into Stringer's hair where he reckoned there would be an ear. 'Where's Christie Maclean then and your friend Donovan?'

Stringer gave Samantha a dig with his pencil and said 'In you go. That wraps it up.' Then he turned deliberately. 'They decided to go on alone. Not being students, they're not my care transportwise. Some private scheme of pleasure I'd guess. Also Delacroix and the Ross girl. They packed in early and made their own way.'

He poked his head through the open door and asked, 'Is that right Samantha? You told me that Maclean girl had gone off with her friend.'

'That's so. He was calling up a hire car. Taking her to Keswick City I believe.'

Cain pitched his voice for Stringer's ear alone, 'I don't pretend to know what you're doing. But hear this and hear it good. I'll find out. And if she's gone against her free choice I'll come looking for you. You'd better have the answer or you'll be a gone mind bender.'

Stringer consulted his pad and used the same quiet channel. 'You don't frighten me, Cain. You'd better realize you're out of your class. Make any move you like and watch for the rush to get you in a strait jacket.'

Christie Maclean ought to have appreciated all the inconvenience of it. Lying in a girl shaped tray and covered with a quick set of plaster she was totally immobile.

In fact, her sensory network was out of kilter. To save time on a tight schedule, the team of white coated technicians had wired her up to a sub liminal suggestion field and if asked, she would have said she was with Samantha Jones and Cyril Donovan on the way to Keswick City following a message from Cain to meet with him there.

Beside her at two neighbouring work heads, Delacroix and Brigitta Ross were being processed by the same routine except that the mental feed was fixing a different memory pattern.

A large sweep hand zeroed with a definitive click on the console above her head and a bleep started up. She was cooked.

Working from either side, two careful craftsmen eased out a row of clips and lifted the top section of the mould. It was a tribute for dedication that their first eye was for the cast.

It was A-okay. Even to a neat small mole located a centimetre nor-nor-east of her navel.

Good work deserves recognition and a leading hand with a crewcut and a lapel badge saying *Supervisor* came up to say 'Nice. Very nice. That's a honey.'

The same could be said for the original, making a statement of balanced curves to please any mathematical mind.

But usage is all. Lifting together as though handling a lay figure, they eased her out of the shell and dumped her on a waiting trolley.

The casts were loaded on a gravity conveyer and trundled off to the next assembly point. Christie Maclean, like a spirit separated from her flesh, was wheeled out through a swing door to a white tiled ward with twelve beds and inspected for dust and plaster fragments by an android with *Staff Nurse* on her bib and a camel hair brush in her hand.

No system is ever perfect. Christie Maclean surfaced partially out of her sleep, opened her eyes and said positively 'That tickles.'

She also tried to sit up and got a firm hand on her chest pushing her down.

The android used her free hand, pulled an adhesive electrode strip on a wandering lead from the bulkhead and slapped it on the patient's forehead. It was all over. Christie Maclean stopped struggling. For her money, she had closed her eyes, had an extraordinary sudden impression that she was nude on a hospital bed and then had opened them again to confirm that she was still in the shuttle on the way to Keswick City with Donovan beside her.

Cyril Donovan himself was pacing about an ante room in another part of the complex and was beginning to think that he was on a totally unfruitful mission.

He had gone along with Stringer as part of a deal that was supposed to put him in touch with the highest levels of the Vorticist movement. So far he had seen nobody except an android steward who had fixed him a meal and wheeled in a portable actualiser to keep him up to date with the evening newscasts.

The medium had been all agog about the arrival of a baboon in the Southern Region nature reserve whose managers claimed it could read a simple text presented on flash cards. Given training in the right facial grimaces it was on the way to joining the staff.

With the animal kingdom shoving from below and androids taking it from the top, it looked as though *homo sapiens* was in for a thin time.

Another item showed Eisenberg himself as an inset still, while the newscaster revealed that the busy minister was to entertain six of his inner wheel colleagues to a working weekend at his remote hideout, where they would tackle the rough draft of a policy document on the educational budget for the next decade.

It was an unusual item in its way. Out of character for the recluse who had the reputation of leaving his work at his desk and odd that there were half a dozen otherwise sensible characters prepared to spend a weekend out on a limbo with him.

Donovan resumed his pacing about. He stopped at a picture window and looked out at the enclosed valley. The building he was in completed one side of a square landing area. Opposite was a low stone wall hiding the beck and beyond it the bald side of a sheer rock face. Left and right, stone outbuildings filled the remaining sides.

Closer in, under his window there was a metre-wide water channel, very clear with dark brown fish nosing about in the patches of green weed. Over the roofs he could see the tree line coming in close. If this was all, it was not much. In fact there had to be more plant somewhere to handle the size of the operation. From what Stringer had said they could turn out androids at the rate of fifty a day if pushed.

As an envoy from a major power group, he reckoned he was not being treated right and he came to a sudden decision. He would test the feeling of the meeting by using his feet.

He was through the door and moving along a half-timbered connecting corridor when the way ahead closed abruptly two metres from his face.

It was close enough to make stopping a problem and he fended off from the barrier with his hands.

As he steadied himself a voice from the rear said, 'Is there something I can get for you Mr Donovan?'

It was the steward who had been in before and there was no visible opening to show where he had come from.

'What's keeping Stringer?'

'Mr Stringer has already left.'

Senses sharpened by the action, Donovan was conscious of a small time lag in the conversation. It occurred to him that he was in reality talking to a relay station. What he said was being transmitted and answered elsewhere with the android used as a transmitter.

Unconsciously he raised his voice as though trying to make direct contact. 'I want to know what goes on. Just get somebody along I can talk to.'

'There will not be much longer to wait. The girl has been processed and your car will be brought round. Before you go, Professor Vort himself will see you. Meanwhile, if you would return to the lounge, I will serve drinks.'

Donovan took his glass to the window and watched the fish. It had a tranquillizing effect and it took a voice speaking from mid floor to cue him in that he had a visitor.

There was no doubt about who it was. A tall egg head with light blue, piercing eyes in a brown well-preserved face said, 'Mr Donovan. I am Professor Vort. You must excuse the delay in meeting you, but we are extremely busy at this time. You will want to know a little more about our project. Sit down and I will try to answer some of your questions.'

George Langton sat across from Dr Lyer in the Southern Hemisphere Consulate. His face was impassive and the Levantine, in spite of having a large executive desk in front of him was feeling nervous as a tick. It always worried him to have secret service contacts in the office. He was conscious that while they could leave and melt into the background, he himself was there present with a fixed address and could be picked up at any time.

He broke a silence that had gone on too long, 'I do not like all the use you are making of this place. It was clearly agreed that only special meetings should be held here. Donovan is already late. The travel bureau is not busy at this time. He could be noticed.'

'Relax. He is an experienced operator. He will be careful.'

'I am still not convinced that we have anything to gain from this venture. The Vorticist movement has been quiet for many years. I cannot see it as a revolutionary force of any consequence. I have been long enough in this country to know that extremist groups never win wide popular support. The great mass of the people are too comfortable. They grumble, but it has no serious meaning. It is just a habit. Every referendum shows the same pattern. When it comes to making a decision, they choose the middle way.'

'True. But revolution is never made by the people. Sometimes it looks as though it was, but that is camouflage. Revolution is made by a minority with a powerful idea who manage to control the executive machine.'

'This the Vorticists have not done and do not look like doing in the foreseeable future.'

Langton took out a cigar case and made a ritual of selecting a long panatella. When the smoke was wreathing round his head, he said, 'You could be right. But it has to be checked out. Reports from a number of agents suggested that the movement was becoming more active and that some major development was expected. K branch sent Cain here. That must mean something. He has had important assignments in the past.'

A subdued blip started up on Lyer's console. Langton pursed his lips and blew out a long blue plume. Lyer said, 'Good. He has arrived. I hope this will soon be concluded.'

There was a stage wait of a minute and a half before the door opened and Cyril Donovan was ushered in by one of the consulate staff who got a nod from his chief and padded out again closing the door quietly at his back.

Langton waited for the soft click of the latch and said, 'Well?'

Cyril Donovan could have said that it was all right for some and that he was only waiting for the day when he could sit on his tail and ask hard questions.

His hesitation allowed time for a nervous cough from Dr Lyer who also began to say, 'We have been waiting for some time for your report. I would be obliged if . . . '

Langton treated him to a pale stare and lifted his hand to stop him in mid flow and Donovan had the floor again.

Events had moved fast for him and he was not too sure of his ground. From the moment he had taken off from Vort's pad with Christie Maclean, he had been convinced that any claim the Vorticist leader made could be substantiated —but he couldn't begin to understand the method.

Three minutes after take off she had cracked into life as though there had been no break in the sequence.

At Keswick City there had been a message delivered by one of the transport terminal staff with a one hundred per cent credibility loading that Cain was sorry that he couldn't meet her after all, but had gone back to Picton and would contact her again.

Donovan had not believed that any mind fixing could be so efficient. She had no idea that anything out of the way had happened since she had been picked up in the lounge of *The Oak*.

Having no other instructions, he had brought her back to Picton City and left her at her door with nothing said to suggest that she had any memory of the afternoon's chase or anything at all unusual.

He began with the good news. 'Vort is interested. He'll see you at his place tomorrow. He wanted later today, but I didn't know how you would be fixed. As early as you like in the morning. Any time from first light. He works a long day. He doesn't give much away, but from what he said there's a big move pending. He gives the impression that it's all sewn up. He talks as though you'd be negotiating with the president elect of the Atlantic Federation. I can only say that when you talk to him you believe he can do it.'

Langton said, 'It's a far cry from being a clever scientist to being a top politician. What resources does he have?'

'I wasn't allowed to see much. Believe me it's a tight outfit. He has this small self-contained valley. But I got the impression it was only the iceberg tip. I'd say the operational part of the complex was underground.'

Lyer said, 'I don't like it. We've never supported extremist groups before. They're unreliable. More than that, they're unsuccessful. It will all come to nothing and security will be endangered.'

Langton said, 'As the head of the service in this region, I will be the judge of that. One thing interests me. I can see that Donovan here was impressed by the man Vort. There is a chance that his claims can be made good. With our help success is made more likely. The results could be out of all proportion to the effort we put in. The Atlantic Federation could be neutralized for a decade by internal conflicts. That would mean a free hand for Southern Hemisphere to move into disputed territories in North Africa and the Caribbean. Some of the neutrals could be persuaded to lean our way.'

Donovan could see the force of it, but as the only one who had spoken with the *guru*, reckoned he should sound a note of caution. 'That's true, Chief, but when you talk to Vort you'll get the impression that he doesn't count on help from anybody. He has it set up to go alone. I had a feeling that he understood our angle and allowed for it. He's the sort who'd double cross his own aged mother. We'll have to be very careful.'

Too late he realized he was getting a very icy stare. Vort had been hard going. Langton was looking nasty. It was not his day.

Langton said, 'I was at the head of this department when you were a boy. I don't need to be told the rudiments of diplomacy. I will keep the appointment and contact you again through the usual channels. Where is Cain now?'

'He will be in Picton. He came back with the main party. They had a go at rubbing him out, but he has a lot of luck.'

'Just so. Leave him for the time being. He is the sort who likes to have all the facts before he makes a report. Have him kept under watch. If he attempts to leave Picton, he must be stopped. Otherwise he might help us to learn more about Vort.'

The lucky man himself was refreshing his libido from his flask and sitting with his feet up on his desk. Taken all round it had been a poor day. Even on a personal level he was left unsure about Christie Maclean. He had already checked that she was in the room below, but he was hoping that she would make a move to contact him. If she did that it could mean that she had been led off by Donovan on some plausible tack. If not then it was more likely that she had gone along willingly, either because she was in the same league or because she liked his company.

On balance he liked the second proposition least.

There was a tap on the outer door and he felt a surge of optimism. The question was still open. She had come to explain.

He slewed off his chair and crossed the floor in two strides ready to say 'So. Cyril has tossed you aside like a broken plaything and you have decided to come home to your family.' In fact the corridor was overfull of Public Safety details with Lieutenant Billot in the van and Sergeant Suter at his right hand.

Without waiting to be asked, Billot walked right in.

Cain switched his prepared speech and said, 'Come in. Liberty Hall. There's only one chair, but the Sergeant can sit on my bed.'

He was the only speaker. Suter closed the door and stood with his back to it. Billot roamed around, looked in the washroom and the closet and finally sat on the edge of the desk.

Cain tried again, 'Don't think I'm not glad to see you, but I'd be happy to know what you think you're doing. Has somebody fallen out of a window again?'

Billot pulled a memo pad out of his top pocket and read off a note, 'I got a call at eighteen thirty on the nose. From a Federal Park area up north. About damage to property. A scooter to be precise. Removed from where it's owner had put it, driven wildly around and abandoned with a broken lock. The lock was burned out by a laser. So we have an armed hooligan at large.'

'Then I can only hope you track him to his lair.'

'Brown hair, bearded, two metres tall, heavy build. Name given as Robert Cain.'

'Don't tell me. It was your scooter and you were concealed in the pannier with your little book.'

Billot said wearily, 'Don't give me that humorous crap Cain. You'd be surprised how many jokey characters I get to deal with. A complaint is a complaint and when it has chapter and verse it has to be investigated. Where have you been today?'

'With a walking party in the area you mention. Ask the organiser Stringer. Somebody's making a monkey out of the law.'

'I just did that. He says he doesn't know. The party was split up. He wanted to be fair, but he couldn't be sure. He mentioned there was a girl with you.'

'That's right.'

Billot nodded to Suter. 'Go and bring her along Sergeant. But just before you go, we'll have Cain's jacket off. Real slow, Cain. Just slip it off.'

Without looking, Cain could sense that Suter had unshipped his service pistol and was watchful. He unzipped his jacket and unbuckled the harness. 'Is this what you want?'

'That's right. Just drop it on the bed. Now the whole

thing is beginning to look more likely. Wheel her in, Sergeant. We'll have this wrapped up in no time at all.'

Suter was quick. She must have been there all the time behind the posse.

Christie Maclean was pale and set faced wearing a long house coat with a pale purple flower pattern. She stood in the centre of the room and wrinkled her forehead when she looked at Cain as though making an effort to recognize him.

Billot said, 'Is this the man you were with this morning?'

'Yes'—her voice was almost inaudible.

'And what happened?'

'It's difficult to remember exactly. I thought he'd gone mad. Being a medic I tried to humour him until I could get help.'

'You thought he was dangerous?'

'We were separated from the main party and suddenly he grabbed my arm and went off the track, through some marshy ground. I lost my shoes. Then we saw this scooter and he broke open the console. I kept trying to calm him, but it was no good. He made me get on and drove off at some people who were coming along. He was slowing down near a village and I managed to get off.'

'Then you went for help?'

'I met up with other members of the party.'

Cain said, 'Christie. Don't you remember we had a meal at *The Oak*? You've got it all wrong.'

'I had a meal there. With Donovan. Then he brought me back. I'm sorry. You look all right now, but you must have had a brainstorm. I don't want to make trouble for you, but you should have treatment for your own good.'

It was all good convincing stuff and Suter who was near enough to do it, patted her shoulder with fatherly re-assurance, 'Don't let sympathy bother you Miss Maclean. I've seen this type before. Just consider that you're lucky to be well out of it. You could have ended up as a mutilated corpse. He won't worry you again and that's a fact.'

Christie Maclean looked as though she was still trying to puzzle it out. 'I don't understand it. His medical record is fine and there's been no violent incident before. At least, now I come to think of it, there was an unusual sequence the day he arrived. He climbed down to my balcony in a state of nature.'

Billot had heard enough. He slid off the desk and stood up. 'That's it then, Cain. A *prima facie* case for taking you in. Whichever way you look at it, the medicine man ought to have his piece. Just pick up a toothbrush, I guess you can get by without a razor. You won't need any night wear, they'll be issuing you with a seamless shroud.'

Cain tried once more, 'Christie. You know that isn't the truth. Where did you go this afternoon? They've planted all that gobbledegook in your head. Fight it. Get it clear. Remember we were chased over the veldt by Vort's androids. I had to take the scooter to get clear. I stopped by the bridge to fix the siren. You said he wouldn't be insured for riot and civil disorders.'

It was clear to the public safety faction that she was doing her best to make sense of it. Her voice was reluctant, sympathy in it. 'I'm sure you don't know what you did. It's not your fault. The mind can play tricks. The medicentre will sort it out for you. Hallucinations are no big problem any more.'

Cain saw how it would be. They had worked a beauty on him. Anything he said would be suspect. Saying now that he was a fugitive from department K, would bring the biggest laugh of the night.

Another thought struck him. If the Vort outfit was so smart they could have made a quick copy of Christie Maclean. She was not quite the same as normal. There was some electric contact gone that had made her special. This could be the Vort version, duralumin under the hood.

Billot said, 'You're free to go Miss Maclean. Sorry we had to spoil your rest. I guess you needed it. Tomorrow I'll send a car for you and you can make an official statement. Thanks for your help.'

She looked hard at Cain, turned away and Suter, distracted by her ringlet, made a courteous move to open the hatch.

Her house coat had a chunky zip to the hem with a release toggle in the form of a black leather loop.

Cain recalled Delacroix's deft stroke with Samantha and it seemed plain that the whole episode could be restructured at a blow. If he demonstrated that the principle witness was a zombie, he was home and dry.

Moving as the thought crystallized out, he stepped up behind his departing guest and before Billot could intervene had yanked down the runner for a full due.

Christie Maclean reacted strongly having been sensitized by the day's alarms. Aiming to get to sanctuary behind Suter she twisted smartly away. Cain had a firm grip of his toggle and the house coat peeled off and stayed in his hand.

For a breathing space there was a still tableau. Cain saw that in a manner of speaking he had backed a loser. After taking a refreshing shower, the Maclean had slipped into her robe without a thought for the action still to come. She was a surprised nude poised for flight with not a rivet or a rheostat in view.

Suter said, 'Holy Cow, he's at it again,' and shoved his pistol aggressively at Cain's sternum.

Billot said, 'That settles it. Send a man down to the tender for a strait jacket. And pick out a few of these studio prints off of his wall as evidence of his state of mind. He's a sex maniac. What are you playing at, Cain?'

'Believe it or not I had the idea she was an android. Here Chris. Catch. Take your robe. Nothing personal. I thought you'd been got at. You have been got at in plain fact. I hope we can sort that out. If you see Delacroix tell him I want to see him. Have him visit me at the precinct. Just in case I need a friend to contact a lawyer.'

Suter had the jacket and made a skilled job of slipping it over Cain's head considering that two thirds of his attention was elsewhere as Christie Maclean sorted out reversed sleeves and wriggled back into cover.

Listening to the dialogue relayed by the pick up under Cain's bed, Stringer felt all the satisfaction of an early prophet finding his forecast fulfilled in every particular.

He was not given to much smiling, but he allowed himself a quiet ration and Carl Nelson who was with him said nervously, 'What is it Adrian?' Something wrong?'

'Just the opposite. It's not often that events shape up so well. Cain's discredited as a witness. He'll have to work at it to prove who he is. In fact the way that went, he'll spend a lot of time on a therapy couch. He'll be lucky if he gets by without a lobectomy. Still, we should make sure of him. You can put the negro and the girl into circulation with a twenty-four hour monitor. That's important. Not five minutes without a hand at the wheel.'

'I'll see to that. It won't be popular though. The section's worked all hours over the last weeks. They were hoping pressure would ease off.'

'Then you'd better make it clear that the real graft's only just starting. From now on in, it's going to be all go. But when it's over they can write their own appointment. Vort knows who his friends are and he'll be generous. He can also be very nasty. Anybody reneging at this point will spend all the rest of a short life regretting the day.'

'That's all right. You don't need to spell it out to me. They're just getting tired that's all. They're all loyal members of the organization. It would help if they knew there was an end in sight.'

'Well, you can tell them this. V day is not far off. The Cambrian branch is all set to back up Eisenberg. Then we have six in the government inner wheel. After that it's a geometrical progression. Within a week we could be ready to move.'

Carl Snelson said, 'It's a lot to take in. After all these years of work, it's hard to believe that the pay off is just round the corner.'

'You'd better believe it and try to look pleased.'

'There could be civil war. Have you thought of that? Then there'd be so much damage that any scientific programme would be put back a century.'

'Who's going to start a war? We're going in at the top. A simple transfer of effective power. The man in the street won't know the difference. Vort'll get to be president without a shot fired in anger. Then we'll have every executive department under our control. Don't worry Carl. It's all been thought out. Democracy goes into graceful degradation without many mourners. Stick to your printed circuit and get used to the idea of being a viceroy.'

Nelson stood up to go. He still looked like a man convinced against reason.

Stringer watched him out thoughtfully. All good revolutionaries look forward to the first purge and he reckoned he had one for his list. As soon as Nelson could be dispensed with he was for out.

Left alone, Stringer hummed himself a tuneless solo. It was all going very well. He reckoned that in the distribution of honour from a grateful leader, he could count on a provincial governorship at the least. He looked in his mirror. For the new image he might even get his haircut.

Another thought struck him. It would be handy at banquets to have a lithe and personable consort. Now the Maclean girl would do very well. He had watched the preliminary stages of the cast taking sequence. She was a grade A package. A little mental engineering when she was next taken into the unit and she could be persuaded that the sun rose and set in his left earhole.

133

There was nothing needing his immediate attention. He could push that one along a little.

He picked up his intercom and dialled through for Christie Maclean's pad in the female staff sector.

While waiting for her to answer he scribbled a note to the janitor. There was no point in leaving the electronic gear in Cain's bedroom. That could be moved out.

CHAPTER EIGHT

Cain took the ride to the Picton City headquarters in silence.

At the reception desk he filled out a blank and then said, 'Where do I request a person to person talk with the administrator?'

Billot, who had stayed at his side said, 'Now what would you want with him, Cain? It's an open and shut case. Why can't you just relax like a regular criminal and let the law take its course?'

Cain said, 'It's a security angle. Federal level. Just put the wheels at slow ahead.'

'You really are disorientated. Don't you understand, it's Saturday night? The Chief has his life to live. If I pulled him back to the station for every crook trying to stall he'd never fit it in. Tell me what's on your mind.'

Cain said, 'I wouldn't want you to have regrets. This should be a private talk.'

'Nobody has secrets in here. If you have anything to say, say it.'

'Okay. First. I couldn't say much in my room, because they have it bugged. You'll find a broadcasting unit underneath that bouncy girl in the middle. That's why I'd papered the wall. I found the site and dug it out. In case they checked I covered the panel. And there's a pick up in a pod under the bed frame.'

'They. Who's this they?'

'There's a political cell on the campus known as the

Vorticists. They have a big Federal hook up and there's a *putsch* on the way. Could be very soon. Vort himself is master minding it from a private research station in Federal Park Three.'

Billot held up his hand. 'Stop it Cain. For the love of God, credit me with a little sense. I know about the Vorticists. We've done routine checks on their organization. They're harmless. Ninnyhammers to a man. They couldn't organize a good neighbour barbecue. The sooner we get you into medicare the better. Just relax. A few hours from now with a nurse's bib leaning over your cot you'll get a different slant on things.'

'All right then,' Cain fished in his inner pocket and presented his Department K warrant between finger and thumb. 'The administrator will know the drill. Have him contact this department. They'll vouch for me.'

'So you have a Federal Seal. Where did you find that?'

'Like I said, some senior officer only has to use his video.'

Billot handed the tablet back. He was plainly undecided. Rationalizing aloud he said, 'I can believe what I see and hear. I heard that girl and I saw your action which substantiated what she said. There's a sort of mad conviction about what you say now. I'll tell you what we'll do, we'll have Suter go around to your room. If he finds the gear in the wall your credibility takes an up twist. Even then you could have planted it yourself. But if he finds it, I'll call the chief. That's as far as I go. Meanwhile you can sit in the cell of your choice and think out another crazy angle.'

Left alone, Cain went systematically through a succession of fifteen isometric drills. At number eight, standing a pace from a wall doing the flat handed push that had shifted the panel in his study room, he thought that if he was under observation it was going to set the seal on Billot's opinion. They would reckon he was well round the twist.

But it worked its usual therapy. Blood nipping eagerly round its circuits, he felt clear headed and ready for the next thing.

First objective when Fraser's clearance got him out of the brig would be Stringer. That one was having it too easy. He would know what had been done to Christie Maclean and he could get busy putting it right. Delacroix and Brigitta Ross would be a help there to persuade the girl that it was all on the level.

Another train of thought sidetracked him. It was humiliating to the human ego to see that it could so easily be fixed. The android comparison was too close for comfort. If there was nothing in the box except data that could be rearranged at anybody's whim a human being was no better than an android and much less efficient as a living unit. If there was no small place in the mental heap that was out of range of the manipulators, where a man could be said to live, what was the big deal about being alive at all?

Even feeling could be simulated. An android could be programmed for an appreciative glug when shown an oil can.

There was a click at the door and he walked towards it ready to accept any apologies that might be offered and get on his way.

Billot came right in and even before he spoke, Cain knew how it would be.

'You're wasting a lot of my time. Suter found a hole in the wall where you might have kept your piggy bank. Nothing else. Now I'd advise you to co-operate with the medics. Just go along with their treatment and who knows you might be back at your job with Southern Region Actualities in a few months' time. I'll take that Federal card in case it gets into the wrong hands.'

Cain took it out and offered it on his palm. Over Billot's shoulder he could see that a guard with a machine pistol on a shoulder strap had stayed out in the corridor and was leaning on the facing wall looking bored.

As Billot's hand closed on the card Cain gripped the wrist inside the cuff of his tunic. At the same time he dropped on his left knee and brought Billot over his bent head.

Before the man had reached the deck he was lunging forward in a sprint start for the guard outside.

That one gave himself a spring boost off his wall grabbing for his pistol to bring it into aim.

It was a divided programme. If he had stayed put, there would have been time to do it. If he had gone for a hold, Cain would have been delayed long enough for Billot to get himself sorted. As it was, Cain dodged left, checked, came in again from the side and ran him through the open door into his chief who was coming out.

Cain whipped the door shut and the spring lock snapped home. Acoustic engineering was a hundred per cent. The noise of civil war cut off.

From the brief view of Billot's face it was clear enough that every gendarme in the region would be on his tail. It behoved him to make some distance while he could.

The cell block was in the basement. As he remembered it, the elevator came up in the reception area twenty metres behind the desk. He began a deep breathing routine as the cage went up. It would all depend on who was in the lobby.

As the door slid away, he took in the set in a racing scan. There was only one. The duty man was pouring himself a cup of coffee from a brown earthenware jug.

Cain crossed the space at a run, vaulted a low fence with a wicket gate and chopped clinically for the man's bent neck. Then he eased him into his swivel chair and looked at the console. There was a switch labelled ADMIT shoved over to OFF and he pushed it to OPERATE.

Double doors to the street swung clear into the hall. He

walked across forcing himself to keep a slow pace. Outside it was dusk, cool and pleasant with lights coming on in the city.

Stringer would do as a first objective. Shake out a little information and then contact the department with something solid for Fraser to move on. Also the Polytech was not the first place Billot would look unless he was adept at the double think.

He found a line of hire cars waiting for the evening rush and signalled for one to peel off the stick. As its door opened for him there was a siren wail from the public safety ziggurat. The doorman had been found or had raised the alarm himself.

Cain dialled his course on the auto pilot, choosing a route that took him within a hundred metres of the polytech and then continued on into the suburbs. There was not much traffic, the evening flow into the entertainment sector had not got under way.

It was not a long ride, but the hire car was governed to a sedate amble and he was swearing in a monotone before the Gothic frontage showed up.

He used the manual gear to override the programme, slowing the car and bringing it into the lowest flight lane five metres above the square. Then he climbed out to the fender, leaned back inside to shove the level to auto and jumped clear.

Lights in the square were adjusting to the fall in the natural lumen count and visibility was not good. An oldster in an ankle length coat, leaning on a pillar in the porch, watched him up the steps and said, 'Do you know, son, I could of sworn you fell out of that car. It just shows how your eyes can play tricks in a bad light.'

Cain said, 'It's because of alcohol shortage in the brain. You need a long drink. Be my guest.' He passed over a negotiable credit and watched the man shuffle off with an unexpected turn of speed.

Maybe if there was a newscast with an identikit

picture, he would remember the face. But by that time he should be well on with his mission.

He made Stringer's pad in three minutes from the entrance and thumbed the summoning bell. There was no joy. The hairy master mind was either out or deep in contemplation.

Cain weighed up the door. It looked a routine job. He put his hands flat on the panel, took a steady breath and began to push. On the count of six he believed that he would get nowhere and put in a last shove to round off the exercise with muscles cording along his back.

There was a sudden explosive crack and he was in, pushing the whole door bodily ahead of him with long strips of lintel shedding from the hinge plates.

Cain skidded to a halt, caught the door before it fell and readied it to throw at Stringer if he should be about.

But the room was empty. Except for a bouquet of brilliantine. It looked as though the Vorticist had gone out on the town.

He took his door and shored it up in its hole. When Stringer used his key it would fall in and with a bit of luck he might hold on to his key and drop on his face.

A quick search of the console desk produced a neat ladylike laser with a full charge in the butt. He tried it out on the hardware, boring experimental holes where they were likely to do good.

Where he was could be the best place to put in a report to the department. He picked up the video and asked for an outside line.

Without the personal channel of his communicator he could only make a recording in clear to a robot answering service and it would take time for onward transmission, but it would be an ace in the hole if he was picked up again by Billot.

When the voice said 'Credo Packing and Transportation Company, go ahead with your request please'—he said briefly, 'Cain. Expedite. Investigation critical. Make contact with me. Check on Stringer. Vort. Minister Eisenberg. Clear me with Picton City Public Safety. Out.'

He went through to Stringer's balcony and leaned out to look along the face of the building. His own room was in darkness, but there was a light either side. Delacroix was back from his ramble and might have some useful gloss on the action in Federal Park Three.

Cain closed the door behind him. There was not likely to be any gain in searching Stringer's apartment. He traversed to the balcony over F30 and began to go down.

Christie Maclean's window was also lit. Putting business before pleasure he dropped on Delacroix's balcony and looked around for the resident. He was sitting at his desk very still listening to a tape.

After a day out and about, it showed a fine sense of duty. But callous with it. He ought to have been busy finding out what had happened to his neighbour.

Cain rapped on the glass. Delacroix looked up, raised his hand for the visitor to wait and finished his paragraph. Then he stubbed a pause button and took his time to amble over to the hatch.

'What is it, then?'

'I was going to ask you that. How long have you been back?'

'Within the hour.'

'And Brigitta?'

'The same. She had to be back for an evening stint in that bar. Takes a serious view of contract obligations.'

'Where did you get to?'

'All the way.'

'No you fool. Geographically.'

'Tailed along at the end of the column. Found a niche in a little ruin. Very pastoral.'

Maybe it was imagination or maybe it was a sudden change of pace after concentrated action, but Cain felt there was a small but measurable time lag in the conversation. It was as though Delacroix had to think out every reply. What he said was in context and natural enough, but the tiny pause was registering every time on Cain's sensitive ear.

'So you didn't see the android posse chase Chris and me over the hill?'

Again there was the tiny pause. 'You have to be joking.'

'Dead serious. As near as damn it all, dead, period. Chris was taken into Vort's place and given a sub liminal brief. Shopped me good with the local gendarme. But you wouldn't know anything about that?'

'No I wouldn't know anything about that. What are you getting at Cain?'

'Forget it. You're sure they didn't have a go at you? They have some very smart techniques up there.'

'Sure I'm sure. What's the programme now?'

'For me. I have to move on or Billot'll have me inside again. Stringer's going to be too busy to run any small vendettas, so I reckon you should be safe for a while, but watch your step. Take a room in town for a time.'

'What are you going to do?'

'For a start I'm going to call on Chris Maclean. I'd like to find out how permanent this mental interleaving is. I might need your help later on.'

'Whenever you like. Just sound the tocsin or whatever you have in your hand at the time.'

It was Delacroix and it was not Delacroix. There was no precise item to point to for proof. But the nudge of a sixth sense told Cain that the Negro had been got at.

He went out the way he had come in, through the balcony door and Delacroix followed him. The light was still on in Christie Maclean's room, but it was a far cry from the lamp she had said she would burn in the window of the inn like Bess the landlord's daughter.

Cain was tensed, ready to move either way. He was giving Delacroix every chance to show his hand.

There was a small hiss of breath like a quick intake to

signal effort and Cain sidestepped and spun on the ball of his left foot.

In the semi dark Delacroix's face was all eyes and teeth. But there were clues enough to show that it was no genial grin to speed a parting guest. Massive hands were closing on the space lately filled by Cain's neck.

There was time for a flash of certainty. Delacroix would never have been so slow to react. He was not normal. Also he would not have given an advance warning of what he was going to do.

Cain ducked under the waving arms and put a lot of power into a short right hand jab into the diaphragm.

For a breathing second, he believed he had broken his wrist and dislocated his shoulder. His punch bag was a tin man. He might as well have cracked his fist into an oil drum.

The force of it took the android off balance, flailing its arms to give the gyro stabilisers a chance. Cain, with his right arm numb, took Stringer's laser in his left hand and shot point blank in a dropping line from the nape of the neck to the middle of the back.

Some functions went mad as the needle beam wrecked their circuitry. Jaw sagging open, the vocal unit stuck on a recorded laugh. Hands rotated on their wrists tearing the skin sheath. Legs went into an up and down jig like a vaudeville policeman. He was technically dead but still full of disorganized life force.

Cain, forcing his right arm into use, nerves crawling with disgust, frog marched the comedy figure to the rail and tipped him over.

He felt the vibration in the soles of his feet as the heavy body hit the pavement in the square.

He went through into the corridor, massaging feeling back into his right arm, let himself into his own room and looked on a confused scene. Billot's searcher had made a job of it. It was a disaster area.

He picked his way through to his balcony. The light was still on in the room below.

Glad of the chain, he swung out and went down one handed, hanging on the geranium like a fruit bat to look into the room.

Sound was cut off but the action was clear enough. Christie Maclean was being pressured and was fighting a rearguard for the clan motto Virtue mine honour.

She was looking pale and a little confused and had a chair between herself and Stringer. There could be unheard music for a game of who sits last, but Stringer was cutting corners, he hooked the chair away with his foot and went for a direct grab.

As a political thinker and psycho wrangler he had gotten to an omega point where he judged direct action was ultimately to the benefit of all parties in the dialogue.

The noise he was making masked Cain's clumsy drop to the deck and his use of the laser to blast out the catch. He was inside when Christie Maclean, nimble in spite of her muddled thinking, evaded the tackle and slipped past Stringer towards the window.

Stringer whipped round and could have been forgiven for thinking that the excitement was giving him double vision. All the clear areas of his face registered open disbelief.

It was hard on a forward thinking planner. Cain ought to be some kilometres off under lock and key. Paying his taxes like the next man, he reckoned he ought to be able to trust Public Safety to do a job.

Belatedly he grabbed for the chair. He even managed to lift it half way for a swing but Cain took it by the legs, twisted it out of his grip and used it to back him to the nearest wall with the top rail grinding against his throat.

Stringer was no stranger to hair, having more than most, but the bearded face glaring at him over the seat was enough to put him off. Cain said, 'A right little rapist have here. Speak Stringer. What are you at then?'

It was not easy with his Adam's apple under compressive stress, but he said, 'Wait. Put that down and we'll talk it over.'

Cain bared his teeth and put his weight behind the chair. He said, 'The time for talk has long gone. You're a dead pig, Stringer. I'm going to have your eyes bulged out of their holes like any gargoyle.'

It was borne in on Stringer that he was hearing a true thing. Unbelievably he could end here in this little room. Breathing was a full time chore and he wasn't getting enough. Eyes beginning to roll, he jerked out, 'I'll tell you. What do you want to know?'

Cain relaxed pressure a fraction and allowed some air to pass. Stringer's face which had been getting a purple hue, went grey. He said, 'I was putting a proposition to Christie.'

'I could see that.'

'All regular. A pairing application to go on file.'

'What would she want getting a contract with a fat ugly bastard like you?'

'When we take over I shall be an important man. She could have an important position.'

Unexpected support came from the female end. Christie Maclean who had been thumping Cain's back said, 'That's true. He did make a formal offer. I refused and I don't like him, but that's no reason to kill him. Let him go. Both of you go and leave me alone.'

Cain said 'Shut up. Go and sit on your bed and listen. That's not all.'

'I'll ring for the janitor and get you thrown out.'

'Do yourself a favour. Five minutes, then you can call anybody you like.'

She moved round to the side and looked at him, eyes full of doubt. But something was trying to surface. Finally she said, 'All right then, five minutes but I'm being a fool.'

Cain dropped the chair and swung it onto its legs. He said, 'Come forward Stringer, sit down. The floor is yours.

I'll sit on the desk. We can all be comfortable. Some more than others— as is usual in an interrogation sequence. I'm going to bore little holes in you from time to time with this laser, your own by one of those twists that fate has. Just begin by telling Christie here what's making her act up in this uncharacteristic fashion.'

Stringer took out a yellow handkerchief and wiped his face. Cain took casual aim and cut away a strip of cloth from his left shoulder.

It cued in a quick speech. 'You were treated in the unit this afternoon. As a medic you will know the drill. Hypnotic drug. Direct feed into the memory. You were programmed to distrust Cain and forget the sequence where you were chased by android units. This will not mean much to you except as a fact to be understood, because the adjustment is very efficient and is as much a part of your mind as anything else.'

Cain said, 'Not so efficient. She was very dubious about it. You can tinker with cognition, but you haven't gotten around to the affective side. She could *think* it, but she couldn't *feel* it.'

Christie Maclean said, 'I don't go much for being talked about like an idiot child. My feelings are my own. I don't like people with a brutal streak even if it can be proved that it's all in a good cause. What else has been going on that I don't know about?'

'We have copies of many of the personnel here. Field trials have shown that the simulation is exact. They are not detectable. A copy was made of you and could be used to take your place in the medicentre.'

'But it wouldn't know all I know. It couldn't keep it up.'

'There is a refinement which has never previously been developed. The original is kept in the unit and is in contact with the android copy. The whole personality of the subject is available to the copy. The copy is the original in a real sense.'

Cain said, 'What's the point then?'

'The original is wide open to suggestion. The android acts out whatever instruction is fed into the original.'

'Wouldn't it be simpler to persuade the original that you have a reasonable programme? Don't answer that. You haven't a reasonable programme. So this is the big fix. How many of these zombies do you have?'

Stringer hesitated and Cain sent a fine beam into the flesh of his shoulder. There was a gasp. 'Over two hundred.'

'And control facilities for that number?'

'Yes.'

'All at that one centre?'

There was a definite hesitation and Cain raised the laser.

'There are some small temporary units for interim control.'

'Until the originals can be shifted to the centre?'

'Yes.'

'What's the extreme range for control?'

'A thousand kilometres. But that's pushing it. We like to keep within five hundred.'

'So Minister Eisenberg will have to stay on his home patch.'

Stringer looked genuinely startled, 'What do you know about that?'

'Enough.'

Christie Maclean said, 'Now that I have the cue to think back, I can remember something. There was a small ward. I can see it clearly. White tiles. Twelve beds in two rows of six. A nurse leaning over me. A staff nurse. But not human. I remember her hand. She was an android.'

Cain said, 'Hold on to that. It's a positive lead. You can work out the rest. They didn't have you for long enough to make any fundamental changes.'

'But they've gone a long way on technique. I never

heard of any therapist claiming he could isolate specific memories and alter the record.'

Perking up a little at the indirect compliment, Stringer said, 'Professor Vort is a genius. He has identified the location of every mental process. He is able to make a working copy of every part.'

Christie Maclean said hotly, 'And what good does he think that will do him? Does he think that when he assembles all the pieces he has a human being?'

'What else? A mind is the sum of its parts. You're talking about a biological computer.'

'A *biological* computer. That's the key word. A mechanical computer isn't necessarily the same thing at all. He's fallen into a medieval error in logic. They believed that if they could show a close parallel they were on to the same cause and effect. It's a nonsense. Like the twentieth century behaviourists who studied animal reactions and tried to apply the findings to the human situation. The whole is more than the sum of the parts. A man is more than an animal and more than a mechanical marvel.'

It was as good as a seminar and Cain was reluctant to break it up. But he was conscious that time was not on his side. He said, 'Well argued, Mac. But we'll leave it there, if you don't mind. I have work for our fat, hairy friend. Use the video Stringer. Call a long distance hire car for your own use. We'll take a trip. You can introduce me to Vort and I'll hear it from the *guru* his own self. On the way you can tell me where Donovan fits into the scheme. I didn't know Southern Hemisphere Intelligence was in the psycho business.'

For the first time since Cain had materialized on the set, Stringer looked pleased. He tried to hide it, but there was an eager spring in his step as he made for the desk before the invitation had stopped vibrating in the air.

Waiting for the call, he filled in with, 'You'll see what I mean. Vort's no ordinary man. Once you've talked to him, you'll be asking to join the movement.'

'Then it's a pity nobody thought of it before instead of all this crude assassination business.'

Stringer was through on an outside line. He said, 'That's okay. They know me; I have a regular account with the firm. They'll have a car round right away.'

'Fine. We'll go down and wait discreetly in the lobby. Just don't go getting any heroic ideas about dodging off. You wouldn't want your friend Vort to be put to the expense of a commemorative plaque.'

Christie Maclean stood up and said, 'If we're going mountaineering again I'll just change into slacks and a sweater.'

'You're not going anywhere. Billot will be calling. I'm surprised he hasn't shown yet. Tell him you haven't seen me. Be surprised in bed all tousled and appealing.'

He got a direct look and thought there would be an argument. Then she shrugged and sat down again. 'If that's the way you want it.'

'That's the way it has to be. See you. Don't forget to water your geranium.'

When they had gone, she listened at the door until the footsteps died away. Then she picked up the video and called another hire company. She said, 'I want a car right away to pick me up in the avenue behind the Picton Polytech. Within the one fifty kilometre range. Single trip.'

She made a racing change, rummaged in a drawer for a pocket torch and went out along her corridor to the opposite end to use the stairway for the rear of the building.

Eisenberg's villa, at the end of a two kilometre winding track that led into the blind end of a box valley, was well placed for a conference. There was nothing other than the agenda to think about.

Arriving at intervals during the day his six guests

reckoned they had been out of their minds to go along with it.

The Employment and Productivity overlord, Glasman, a wheezy man with a spreading paunch, met his friend Balmer the Minister for the Environment as he stepped from his official shuttle and said, 'Well, Jack. Welcome to Devil's Island. Don't make any quick decision about when you want transport out. By the end of the day we'll all have damp rot in every joint. Staying the night here would be my death.'

Balmer looked at the house front, a low rambling structure with small mullioned windows, black and white daub and wattle carefully restored and a forest of twisted red brick chimneys. 'Don't you have any sense of History? The guide book for these parts says that Elizabeth the First had an illegitimate baby in this house.'

Nobody gets to be Minister without a shrewd streak. Glasman had his finger on the flaw in the argument right away. 'But I'm not having a baby, illegitimate or otherwise.'

'With a belly like yours, Abe, you'll never convince anybody. Who's arrived so far?'

'Just you and me. Eisenberg's here of course, though I haven't seen much of him. I don't like the atmosphere. This place gives me the green creeps. What's his angle? I don't get it.'

'You have an agenda.'

'Integrating training schemes with requirements for the next decade. He could have asked a computer.'

'We'll just have to wait and see. He's a close one. But he has the makings of a future president. You can't pass up an opportunity to be in on the ground floor. When he's counting his friends on his fingers he'll remember this day.'

As they reached the low Tudor door, another shuttle, a military craft with the North Atlantic blazon of a blue and white hemisphere surrounded by olive branches, stormed up the valley, hovered over the apron and dropped neatly between a flower bed and a fountain. Two tall figures stepped out and looked around. Fergus and Quale, Public Safety and Federal Defence.

Balmer said, 'Now you can feel safe. Have the General as a godfather.'

'Who have we still to come?'

'Health and Public Works.'

'Mercer and Jordon. It makes a pattern.'

'Surely it makes a pattern. We all have an interest in how many people are trained for what.'

'Not only that. Not one of us aligned permanently with any major party.'

'So that shows his good sense. If he gets six in his corner he's on his way. Keep an open mind.'

'Well there's nothing to lose.'

'That's it. That's it precisely.'

Lunch set in a long dining room with a view down the valley brought a more cheerful frame of mind. Eisenberg was going out of his way on a PR kick to be all things to all men. Smiling a lot, eating little himself for fear of overloading his disposal bin, playing the country squire.

Finally he produced a squat bottle from a cupboard in his sideboard and said, 'This is something special, gentlemen. Nothing artificial about this. I'd like you to give me your opinion. We will drink to the success of our meeting.'

He made a tour of the table charging the glasses with his own hand, returned to his place and said, 'To a better future.'

None were doing too badly in the present. But everyone looks for improvement. He got a murmured response and every glass was emptied. Dr Mercer, a specialist in flavours, even said 'A noble liquor, Minister,' before he dropped the glass and went rigid in his seat.

A philosophical observer might have said that in the country of the blind, the one-eyed man is king. There was none present. The two serving wenches in Tudor dress who had added their mite to the homely ambience had been treated to a shot of tranquilliser apiece as they leaned over the sink in the old world kitchen by one of Eisenberg's attendant androids.

But it was true enough that Eisenberg, moving round the table checking the reflexes of his silent guests was far and away the most human looking figure on the set.

He completed the tour and stopped as though in thought. Vort, monitoring this crucial phase, cut in with direct instructions. Android staff filed in and began to carry out the sleepers to a mobile lab parked at the back of the house. It had been designed to take six in communication stalls.

Temporary models of the diners walked in and took their seats. Refinements could be made against the originals. It was a neat and tidy operation.

The two girls straightened from their sink and one said, 'You know Gwyneth, I could of sworn some lecherous swine took a sly nip. This place has a bad reputation. I'd never stay here overnight. Haunted by a man two and a half metres tall they say it is.'

'I never saw a man two and half metres tall. I wouldn't like to neither. I felt something too. Maybe he was in here with his big pinching fingers.'

A bell jangled on a room indicator. 'That's them. They've finished. We can clear away. I tell you I'll be glad to get back to the village. How is it they don't want us again?'

'There's a caterer coming in from Wrexham City to do the evening meal and then there's only breakfast. They'll be away back South before midday.'

'And no loss. Still it's interesting to see public figures at close quarters. Just goes to show they're no different from anybody else. In fact that fat one was giving me some very ordinary looks.'

'Maybe he's a reincarnation of Henry the Eighth. That Tudor rig switched him on.'

'Well he can just switch himself off again.'

The room was empty. The visitors could be seen through the windows taking a turn round the rose garden. Any newshound with a telescanner could get a picture for his album.

There was even conversation going on as Vort, watching through Eisenberg's eyes and listening through his aural receptors, tried out his new puppets on a link up with the mobile lab.

It was good, but clumsy at the distance. He told Eisenberg to have the lab take off and bring the catch to base. In the interim, the politicians could have a siesta.

Count down to the ultimate pay off was on the way.

CHAPTER NINE

Except for a pool of light round *The Oak* and a pale nimbus behind the trees surrounding Vort's place; the valley was in darkness when Cain's hire car rounded the bluff for the home run.

Cain said, 'I take it you're well known to the two gribbles who guard the gate. Just say whatever has to be said to get us through. Be selfish. Just think that any chance remark could be your last.'

It was Alf on duty and he peered into the plexidome with his long face spread further by the curve. Stringer dropped the panel and a night smell compounded of peat and fir resin drifted in. He said, 'It's me, Alf. Just clear us with the house.'

'This is not your usual time, Mr Stringer.'

'No, something came up unexpectedly.'

'What time will you be wanting to leave? I usually lock up at twenty-three hundred.'

'It's getting near that now. Just carry on. We'll very likely stay overnight.'

The roadway bore right through the trees, skirted a mill pond, passed a row of stone cottages and dipped steeply to a clearing by the beck. Floodlights clewed to the walls of outbuildings made it as light as day.

Stringer ran into a space between a silver long distance shuttle and a large transporter that looked like a field hospital unit, killed the motor and climbed out. He was looking much more cheerful and Cain reckoned soberly that he had every right. He was on his own dunghill.

They crossed the courtyard with Stringer a pace ahead and an android with a plain gun metal head, micro grooved to give a shifting illusion of regular features, slid back a panel at the left hand corner of the principal building.

There was no visible cake hole, but his voice did all right beamed from the mouth area and saying, 'Come in Mr Stringer. What can I do for you?'

'Just pass the word along that I'm here. This is Mr Cain. If it is possible, he would like to see Professor Vort.'

'That may not be easy at this time. He is working in the operations sector. Please wait in the reception room. I will see that he is informed.'

Stringer, gaining confidence all the time, wheeled out a drinks trolley and poured himself a long drink. Cain settled for a beer and carried it to the window. The fish were still moving about, stimulated by the light. It was all very rural and ordinary. There was even a sense of anticlimax. Vort, if he turned out at all, was going to be a high minded senior citizen, working for humanity, incredulous that any dim ape should suspect his motives.

Stringer, fortified by his drink, said, 'What pleases me Cain, is that you did it all by yourself. Couldn't wait to get here. Forced me to bring you. I hope you'll think of that in the fullness of time.'

'Keep your delight to yourself. It isn't too late for you to get a hole in your gut and have all that good liquor wasted. This is a very small outfit for the scale of the enterprise.'

'I can tell you this, because it won't go any further. What you see is only the ground installation. All the operations complex is underneath. Spreads away under the hill there. All the construction work was done from the quarry. There isn't a better equipped dianetics lab anywhere in the world.'

'But what do you have to gain? Let's just suppose that it

all works out and you put a whole raft of android replacements in the field, get your party in power even, you haven't altered a thing. You're still Adrian Stringer, peering out from under a bush. You can't eat any more or drink any more or wear more than one hat at a time—always supposing you could get one on.'

Answer, when it came, was from another source as though Stringer had developed ventriloquist powers.

'What you say, Cain, is true in part, but it misses out an important factor. A man must try to go as far as he can along the path of his vision. Your philosophy is only for baboons.'

They had gotten an addition to the duologue. There was no doubt in Cain's mind that it was Vort himself. The voice was smooth and cultured. When he tracked it down to its owner he found a tall nut brown mandarin type with light blue eyes, wearing a white fluted tabard of stiff metal cloth with a Phoenix in gold wire on the centre panel.

The man had used his name so the bush telegraph had been busy. He had also come at once which meant he knew something about Cain's reason for being interested. Also he was confident that there was no threat in it.

The ideas had presented themselves all at once in Cain's head. He was still sorting them in a value order when Vort spoke again. He had gotten in first and it was uncanny. 'You are employed by department K. Naturally I want to know first hand why you are here. You are either very brave or very foolish. That I shall find out. I hope you will not try anything rash, because the consequences would be serious for you.'

'Let's say I object to being pushed about by amateurs. The jig is up, Vort. Department K will want to know a lot of answers and it won't help if I don't give them personally.'

'We can arrange that. It will be no trouble to send an exact copy to make a report. In fact it will also give your resignation. Then you will quietly disappear. I'm afraid your intervention has done you no good at all.'

Stringer, looking very pleased, said, 'I tried to convince him of that, but it was no good.'

'I'm sure you did. But what has happened is probably for the best, though it is a pity it has given you this unnecessary journey.'

Cain felt the initiative was slipping away. He unshipped the laser and held it in a relaxed, matter of fact way, aiming nowhere in particular. He said, 'One item not on your schedule is the plain fact that I don't give a fractional damn for either of you. Tell me what you're supposed to be doing here Vort, or your curious career is going to meet a full stop.'

Stringer was looking nervous again but Vort was unmoved. He said 'You must think I am very naïve to meet an armed man without protection. Throw your pistol down, it is no good to you.'

Cain said, 'We can always try,' and sent a short burst for Vort's shoulder.

The needle thin beam made visible by tracer elements was dead true and on target for half the way across the room. Then it splayed out in a brilliant asterisk.

Vort's lips moved in a social smile though it stopped short of the eyes. They were ice cold. He said, 'You see. You are outclassed here.'

There had been no visible signal but the android orderly appeared at the door. Vort said, 'Now I will advise you again to throw down your gun.'

Cain shrugged. The man had a point. He remembered a louvre ventilation system in the window behind him and shoved the laser through a gap. It dropped and made a splash, scaring a fish into a sudden spasm. It was better there than picked up by Stringer who might get ideas above his station.

'So there it goes. It makes no difference. I still want to know what you do here. Knocking off a parcel of students is one thing, but knocking me off would be another. Your private affairs are about to become public; make no mistake about that.'

'In a sense you are right. But the time and the method are of my choosing. Since you are so curious you shall see for yourself. See from the inside. Follow me.'

They backtracked along the entrance corridor and passed the courtyard door on the left. Trying to keep orientation Cain judged they turned through a right angle towards the quarry before they took an elevator for a short drop of some ten or fifteen metres. Then they went on in the same direction on a walkway that began to move as soon as their weight came on it.

Timing against speed Cain reckoned three hundred metres with a slow drop of another twenty in depth below the surface. That would put them under the quarry itself.

Vort said, 'Quite right Cain. You are under the quarry,' and there was no longer any doubt that in addition to any other refinements he was working a smart number in ESP.

Now there was more evidence of the scale of the operation. The underground complex had branching avenues every whichway with walkways, an overhead monorail for freight handling and signposts to keep confusion at bay.

There was also a fair measure of activity, workers in white coveralls nipping about, some recognizable as androids with the microgrooved ovoid headpiece. How many others had a tin core was anybody's guess.

The walkway took a right fork and there was a succession of double swing doors on either side. Labels said *Trade, Finance, Public Safety, Military, Regional Government*.

Without making any movement that could be identified, Vort flipped some sensitive relay and they stopped, facing *Political Control*.

158

'I suppose this is a vanity I should have outgrown, but I would like you to see the first major breakthrough of the enterprise. Then you will understand the futility of opposition. Not that I am offering you a place in the organization, we have enough simple minded, strong arm units. But it will be a first step in making your mind more pliable and open to suggestion.'

Cain said, 'One thing I'll say to you, Vort. You're the original big head. It ought to frighten you. You're a sucker for *hubris*. Those that the gods would destroy they first make mad.'

It earned him a very cold stare. Vort hesitated as though about to speak and then motioned for him to go first through the hatch.

Inside there was brilliant shadowless light, white tiled walls, a long room maybe seventy-five metres by fifteen broad.

One wall had a continuous computer spread with work heads for a dozen operators, all manned by white coated figures. The opposite wall was spaced out by couches at a thirty degree slope. There was accommodation for twenty-five, but only seven were occupied and each one had an attendant. Seven identical prototype Florence Nightingale figures with round friendly faces, well filled bibs, fair hair and elegant legs. No patient was going to beef that his neighbour had a nicer nurse. It was democracy in action.

Cain read off the label over the first bed. It said 'J. BALMER. ENVIRONMENT'. He knew the name and recalled seeing the Minister in newscasts. But not in a state of nature with electrodes clamped by suction pads to every major centre and wearing a round shiny dome well down on his forehead.

He went down the line, Glasman, pale and fat, Mercer, Jordon, Fergus, Quale with a lifebuoy tattooed round his navel, a relic of the soldier's life. Last in line was Eisenberg, ascetic as a prophet.

They were all still as wax. Across the floor seven

scanners showed pictures of different rooms as though seen through the eyes of a person in them. Cain had done the sum before Vort said, 'You are looking at the scenes which the replacements see. Every item is transmitted back. It is virtually seen by the original here. He reacts to it as though he was present. But his reaction is monitored and modified according to what he is needed to do. That way the replacement unit has all the knowledge and behaviour pattern of the original. Indeed it could be said to be the same man acting at a distance from himself with guidance from a controlling hand.'

'So what? You can do it for seven and for all I know you can do it for a hundred, but you can't do it for a whole population. And if you could, what would be the point? You're playing a game of toy soldiers. Grow up, Vort. Come out into the world and tackle it direct instead of one move out from reality. It's all very clever, but it doesn't give anybody an extra breakfast egg or a clean pair of socks.'

'You miss the point. This is the nucleus of a silent revolution which will transfer power to the Vorticist movement. Effective power has always been in the hands of a few, whatever democratic trappings have been paraded in front of the people. In a few months the process will be complete and will be irreversible.'

'I still don't see the point. Who gains what? To invoke that old gag about the pursuit of happiness, who gets to be happier? A prime case of megalomania like yourself wouldn't recognize ecstasy if it was served up on a flat dish.'

'I am concerned that mind should reach out to its ultimate fulfilment. It is time for a new leap forward comparable to the step that was made when biological man became conscious of his own identity.'

Cain said, 'I'll tell the department that you're a benefactor at heart and maybe they'll overlook this rough play that you get up to. You can plead insanity and get to live out your days in a comfortable asylum with a few electronic bits and pieces to play with.'

He was walking away from Vort, wheeled suddenly and dived in for a hold, reckoning that if he got Vort's neck in a convincing lock he might even up the ante.

He was within centimetres of a touch. Vort's eyes had not blinked or lost their icy blue stare. Black night filled his head as though a dark tide had sluiced in. He was unconscious before his momentum carried him spread-eagled to the floor.

Christie Maclean left her shuttle at *The Oak* and walked up the road in near pitch darkness. Once she had turned the corner out of sight of the village, she could have been anywhere black, overhung with foliage, with an oppressive sense of land piled up at either hand and a plantation smell. It could have been any time since the first lung fish crawled out of the sea. She felt utterly alone, beaten back into the small clearing of her own mind with primal chaos all around.

Even there privacy had no guarantee. According to Cain and Stringer there had already been an invasion of her head. It could be true. A residue of the mental plant was still telling her that Bob Cain was false as water. Even the evidence she had at first hand was against him. He was a professional double dealer.

But the biological trap had been sprung at another level. She did not want to believe it, or at least that the double dealing was continued on a personal level. It was very confusing and as an independent professional type, she reckoned she should find out for herself.

In some ways the confusion was a help. It got her along the track without too much brooding about the vulnerable situation she was in.

Moving quietly on foam soled sneakers she reached the lodge. A single light burned in an upper window. Eyes adjusted to the low lumen count, she could see that the archway was sealed off by a massive grille.

Like Cain, she went on, following the line of the wall until it turned off the road.

She crossed the paddock and used her hand torch briefly to read the caption over the arch where the beck went into its culvert. Instinctively she felt that it was too easy. Nobody was going to bar the front door and leave a hole in the wall.

She followed the stream until it was shallow and littered with boulders, then she balance walked across without getting her feet wet.

The slope was an easy scramble and as she reached the top a three quarter moon came out as a bonus for a trier.

Fifty metres off, the quarry fence was stark and plain with its insulators carrying their own message.

It was a big disappointment. She must have been stupid to expect to walk right in. She was no nearer. Staying in Picton would have been more sensible.

The sheer frustration of it cleared her head. Confusion sorted itself out. Conviction that Cain was right grew and established itself as a positive force.

Anything so secretive had to be wrong.

She went up onto higher ground and was looking down a slope to the fence. Concentrating on it, she caught her foot in an overgrown rail and came down full length.

It was an ancient mineral track that had once served the quarry, probably to take out spoil for dumping.

She followed it and found a crazy timber platform with a rusted tipping truck run out to an overhang.

Nerves crawling with *angst* she imagined that it might have started on its downward journey while she was lying across the track and gone plunging on to a frenzied suicide in the distant quarry.

Blocks of slate were chocked against the wheels. Probably it wouldn't move if they were shifted.

Then she was looking around for a lever. Vort's

palisade was a symbol of his personality. He thought he was bomb proof. Maybe she could cut a hole in it.

In cold blood she would never have done it, but she suddenly saw the flash scene of the small ward and the android leaning over her bed. A dried branch broke at the first attempt. A fence picket stood the strain and she painstakingly set up a small cairn to act as a fulcrum for purchase.

With the first slab shoved over she repeated the drill at the other side. It was a heavier stone and she had to swing every gramme of weight and strength into it.

The picket broke with a pistol crack and she lost her footing, rolling off the platform and clawing for a hold to keep her from a long drop into the beck.

Small trash cascaded around as she scrambled to the lip and the noise of it concealed what was happening up top.

The massive truck was on the move. Slowly at first, groaning at every rusted bearing, shaking the decayed timbers, it was on its way.

Christie Maclean, streaked with sweat and dust, hauled herself to solid ground and watched its progress in the moonlight.

Swaying from side to side, screeching like a banshee it left the end of its track and ran on over clear stony ground for the fence. When it hit, there was a flash of eye-aching light and an explosion that sent a savage tremor through the ground.

Lines of blue fire flared and wreathed as wires coiled and snaked away spitting to earth.

The truck ploughed through, glowing incandescent, loose plates flapping, a grotesque phoenix, ran on for a hundred metres, carving the corner from an old lofty shack and then dipped away out of sight. The firework display blacked abruptly.

Christie Maclean hauled herself soberly to her feet. There was the sound of a distant splash and a continuing silence.

If she wanted to get in, the way was open. Facing it squarely she thought it was about the last thing she wanted to do.

It would have helped if there had been a cutting out party rising from the heather shouting Death or Life and a piper sounding. But Cain was inside somewhere and if he could do it, she could do it.

She found she was inside the fence running toward the building that the runaway truck had breached.

As she reached the broken corner there was the rattle of a metallic shutter lifting away. The whole side of one of the outbuildings had rolled up. A flat toast rack personnel carrier nosed out and ran over to the broken fence.

At least a dozen figures spilled out. Termites come to repair the nest. The moonlight was reflected on bland faceless domes. Androids all.

Half the force began to heave out tools. The rest fanned out for a search of the area carving up the shadows with powerful hand lamps.

Inside the building was the best bet. But a metre from the opening, her hands met a smooth wall. It was out of character. A new structure within the old shell. A curved surface like a well head.

She followed it round and chanced a narrow beam from her torch. It was a cylinder running up to the full height of the building with a narrow gallery round the top.

A duralumin ladder clewed to the side led to the top. She shoved the torch in her waist band and started up.

As she reached the gallery and stepped on to it over a half metre parapet, there was a scuff of footsteps from the broken wall. There was time to lie down flat and the roof above her head was picked out in sleazy detail as a beam shone up from below.

Another pair of feet picked their way through the gap and a flat functional voice, 'Go up. I will stay here.'

Crawling on hands and knees, Christie Maclean moved quietly to the far side.

There was another ladder, two metres of it to the lip of the shaft where there was a gap between the top of the wall and a fluted cowling supported on short tubular rods. Maybe she could hang inside.

Only the memory of the blank ovoid heads would have made it possible. Leaning out over the rim she shone her torch down. It was lost in distance but a system of broad lugs went away from where she was and every ten metres or so there was a round platform with a guard rail.

It was just possible if she went below the first one she would be out of direct vision.

There was a solid knock as the android left his ladder for the gallery and it needled her to move on. Hands beginning to sweat, she twisted out over the drop and climbed down.

She heard the android make a circuit and could even see his elongated shadow on the roof of the cowling. He called down 'Nothing here,' and got the reply, 'Check inside the shaft.'

It was all right for some. Even androids had other androids calling the shots.

Working to the extreme edge of the rungs with her head touching the platform, she waited for the pay off. Light flooded down the shaft, held for a long count of six and the voice echoed down the well 'All clear.'

'Stay on the gallery out of sight in case anybody tries to reach it.'

'Very well.'

She went slowly down to the next platform and rested with her feet through the hole and her back to the rail. The air was warm and stale. It must be some kind of ventilation shaft. So there was something to ventilate. Androids would not be particular. Only people liked their ration of fresh air.

She said, 'Maclean, why do you think? You are a fool

to yourself,' and started slowly to find the first rung.

At the beginning, she counted platforms resting every five. But she had lost count when her feet hit rock bottom and she could actually stand and lean on the shaft wall. There was still a faint glimmer of light at the top of the tube, an immense distance off.

Close at hand there was a greying of the darkness in four circular areas spaced round the shaft. She used the torch again. Outlet flues a metre and a half in diameter were closed off by fine mesh filters and diffused light came from behind them.

The screens were a detachable fitting clamped to a housing by three knock over clips. Standing close, she could feel the warm draught blowing through.

Maintenance was a regular feature, the clips shifted under finger pressure and she lifted one of the screens away and laid it flat on the deck. Now the light was stronger and it came from the sides of the flue at intervals until it curved away twenty metres ahead.

Curiosity, that doubtful handmaid of evolution, drove her on. There was room to walk, head well bent. The first light source was a common room of some kind. Not too well lit. Probably a low power feed was on after the electric storm at the fence. She went on. Store rooms. A dining area—so they were not all mechanical marvels. A dispensary. An android park with rows of still figures waiting for the resurrection word. A moulding plant of some kind, working late. A still figure being wheeled in on a trolley.

As it came close she recognized the beard. It was Cain and to all intents and purposes he was dead.

Christie Maclean stretched one leg at a time and massaged the back of her neck. In theory there was room to lie down and be comfortable, but she had been drawn to her restricted window on the world where she could only kneel or crouch, feeling that if she took her eyes off the scene she could miss a major development.

Cain stayed still. His two attendants were clearly waiting for a signal.

Her watch told her she had been there an hour, but it could have been a week.

Footsteps below stopped her therapeutic ploy. A voice with a recognizable human timbre said, 'Full power will be restored to this section at 0200. Meanwhile you can join the team in the preparation room.'

A doctor type with a hatchet face, going thin on the crown, wearing a white coat, came into view, leaned casually over the trolley and flipped back one of the sleeper's eyelids. He seemed to be satisfied with the view and pushed off the way he had come.

The two androids left by another door and Cain had the set to himself.

She waited two minutes by the clock. There was no sound. Working quietly she eased out the ventilation grid clips and lifted the panel into the duct.

Shoving out her head and half expecting it to be hit by a club, she looked around.

The door the doctor had used was over left in her own wall. There was a second almost opposite and a third beyond Cain's bed. Below her was a large white enamelled storage cabinet and she wriggled out of her hole to stand on its top.

Cain, when she reached him was still a lay figure and she was suddenly out of programme. He was too heavy to move.

She put her head on his chest and listened to the heart beat. It was powerful and regular.

If the trolley had been wider she would have climbed in beside him and gone to sleep. As it was she leaned over him, a hand on the rail at either side and spoke softly but urgently into his ear. 'Bob. For godsake. Snap out of it.'

Reaction was small on a cosmic scale, but so unexpected she let out a startled 'Eek.'

Cain's eyes flicked open, focused on the face ten centimetres off and widened with simple pleasure. He obviously thought it was the best thing he had seen in a long time.

There was a moment of balance, a loaded silence with positions taken and freely accepted in a mental sense with an earnest of practical measures to be taken if and when there was a time to come.

Cain's hands went to the sides of her head, fingers probing through hair like fine silk. Then he bent his arms and pulled her in for a brief confirmative seal on a bargain already struck.

Christie Maclean said, 'They'll be back. There's a power failure on. We have to get out.'

Cain swung himself off his narrow bed, stood swaying, and she had to catch him before he fell. He said thickly 'Give me a minute.'

There was a sink let into a work table and she got him over to it. Ice cold water gushed from a faucet and he splashed handfuls of it over his face and chest, shaking his head like a wet dog.

It was time consuming, but it was doing good. He was feeling better all the time. The noise he was making masked the opening of the door and the doctor was well inside on the way to slip in a booster shot to keep his patient tranquil.

He had the hypo all ready, carrying it upright in a practised hand.

The nudge of a sixth sense had Cain spinning round from his sink. Surprise held the medico still for a crucial second. Then he was away like a rabbit for his hole.

Cain caught him with his hand on the latch, took the wrist holding the hypo in a bone crushing grip and wrapped an arm round his neck. He also said in a convincing snarl, 'Make a sound and your head leaves its stalk.'

He walked the man over to the trolley and sat him on it. 'Chris. Pick your spot and give this gribble a few ccs of the magic potion. It's a pity to waste it.'

'I'm not sure that it isn't against the Hippocratic Oath.'

'Don't mess about, I'm on a cold floor.'

She took the hypo, rolled back a sleeve and made a neat job of it. The man went slack.

Cain spread him on the trolley and zipped off his coat.

They were built to a different specification and the coat would only fasten half way, but the thick soled creepers were a unisize elastic job and he felt more at home on the sophisticated set when he had them on.

He finished stripping the medico and laid him out flat.

Christie Maclean said, 'Won't they recognize him as soon as they come in?'

'They who?'

'Two androids. I heard him say they would be able to get on with whatever they had to do at 0200.'

'Maybe not. If they're programmed to a single process they won't care who it is. Could be their own mother and they wouldn't bat an eye.'

'Androids don't have a mother.'

'You surely haven't come all this way to split hairs. How did you get in?'

'Through that ventilator. It leads to a long air shaft that comes out in the quarry.'

'Let's go then.'

He lifted her through and pulled himself in after her. When the screen was in place, the house lights below brightened as if a stage hand had shifted a dimmer.

Christie Maclean was thinking that if you had to be in an air duct and personally she could take it or leave it, there was a lot to be said for company.

Cain took her hand, which was pleasant, but he was

only looking at her watch. It was coming up to 0200.

Slap on cue the two androids returned to duty. Without a pause they went into their routine. They prepared a base, rolled the trolley over to it, lifted the still figure onto the soft bed and began to cover him from the feet with round malleable gobbets of special plastic.

Cain gave a thumbs up signal with his free hand and they moved silently away. It was an object lesson in specialization. They were fixed to make the best cast they could and they would do it come wind come weather. What they were copying was strictly for the birds.

At the foot of the shaft they stopped. It was pitch dark aloft and the beam of Christie's torch was lost in distance.

Cain said, 'You've got a nerve Mac, climbing down here.'

'I didn't have much choice, there was a search party closing in.'

'Don't spoil it. I want to think you did it to find me.'

'If I confessed to that I'd be in an impossible position with no room for manoeuvre.'

'All positions are relative but some are more productive than others.'

'What's that supposed to mean?'

She was playing for time on several fronts and lost out on one when Cain said, 'Go first and I shall have the pleasure of catching you if you miss a grip.'

'Do we have to start right away?'

'As of now.'

'I'm not sure it was such a good idea getting you off of that slab. Time was when I could please myself.'

She climbed to the first rung and Cain closed in behind her, hands stretched outside her, head pressing in the small of her back, a warm reredos, damping down a small muscular twitch that had started up in her left thigh. He carried on the therapy by saying, 'You feel good. Backed like a salmon, as your Scottish bard has it.'

'A fishy compliment.'

'What do you expect at the bottom of a ventilation shaft? Get moving.'

The first fifty metres was not bad and they made good time. Then knowledge of the growing distance to the deck made it harder. Already tired she was gripping too hard and using more strength than was necessary. At a hundred metres they took a spell, sitting on the small platform backs to the rail.

She said, 'I've just thought. There's still a big problem when we get out. They'll have repaired the fence and probably left a guard. How do we get out?'

'Getting out is always easier than getting in. People who plan a defence system look at it from the inside. They're so busy putting themselves in the position of somebody outside trying to get in, they never consider the freak case of an insider trying to get out.'

'That's official?'

'It's in the handbook.'

'Okay.'

'Ready to go on?'

'No. But I'm wholly tired of this shaft. Let's go.'

It was slower. Time standing still. Only the necessity to reach for the next rung, climb and reach again.

When they made the platform before the top, she believed that it had been going on for ever and that there had never been anything else in her life but a succession of rungs. When Cain said 'Wait', she sat on the step with one arm hooked through a rail and her mind as blank as the darkness.

Cain went silently up the last pitch, pulled himself through the bars and found the outside ladder.

It was not completely dark. Moonlight was coming in through the shattered corner and the gallery was just visible.

He was two rungs down the ladder when he heard a slow step from the far side. He dropped the last two metres sliding his hands down the rails. The movement was coming from the left so he moved right.

A light flashed on turning the set to bright day, but he was out of sight round the curve.

The android quickened its pace, following its sensors and missed out on elementary human judgement. Cain came up behind and had its head in a lock before it's data acquisition network had done the sum.

Fine rivets popped against his arms. He levered back with a total concentration of power that lifted the ovoid dome out of its seating and broke it free with a trail of ripped out leads.

The headless trunk still powered by an independent motor broke free and followed the last order from the executive end.

He left it walking round the gallery and climbed up to call to Christie Maclean.

'All clear. You can come up.'

Waiting for her, he caught the mobile torso on its next round and took a hand gun from its equipment belt. As an afterthought, he tucked the severed head in the crook of its arm.

The old equaliser had a comfortable feel.

When Christie Maclean appeared through the bars he reckoned he was ahead on all counts.

CHAPTER TEN

Cain stood in the broken corner of the ventilation shaft building with his left hand comfortably sited on Christie Maclean's hip and the hand gun in his right. Up aloft, there was a steady shuffle as the android carried its head in a tireless circle of the gallery.

First light was spreading from the East. The abandoned quarry looked like an industrial slum, a gaunt wasteland. A dawn wind gusted about, heralding rain.

The maintenance crew had long finished the repair job on the fence. It was intact again with a fifty metre section of new wire giving off a high lustre shine.

Christie Maclean, lips brushing his ear, asked, 'Where are they, then?'

'Still around or they'd have called off the headless wonder.'

'What do we do now?'

'On your knees like a ginger rabbit and follow me.'

Cain crawled along the footings to the next corner and lay flat. If they were posted around they would be scanning the set for something at eye level.

Ten metres off, the old surface road that led from the entrance near the village wound its way round the rim of the quarry and lay in shadow in a gulley.

He moved slowly, nerves crawling for the challenge, reached a stone revetment and dropped a metre to the road itself.

Christie Maclean followed over the edge and slithered forward onto his hands.

Fifty metres bent double and the cutting was deep enough to walk upright without poking up against the skyline. Mist filled the roadway rolling in suddenly like a low cloud, bringing fine rain.

Cain said 'Marvellous. Couldn't be better.'

Christie Maclean shivered, 'Oh sure. Now they don't know where we are and we don't know where they are, so it's all even.'

The road was steeper, heavily ridged to give transporters a grip. They went down for a hundred metres and Cain judged they must be nearing the gate.

He was trying to remember what it had looked like from the outside when the mist rolled clear as quickly as it had come. It was all there. The gate with its notice boards, the road beyond it, a lodge built of slate blocks partly let into the hillside and an android guard with a wet shine on its ovoid head standing against the near wall looking up the road.

Cain was moving before the scene had settled definitively on his retina, mobilizing every atom of urge into a weaving run that covered the twenty metres in a personal record for the distance.

The android had two instructions on its tape. One was to report movement and the other was to exterminate any human intruder. Confused by the mist, it was too long making up its mind. Cain reached it as it sorted the order and came down on the side of shooting first and reporting later.

It had made a non-repeatable error. Cain was inside its air space deflecting the blaster with his left forearm and shoving the heel of his right hand under the notional chin, slamming its head through ten centimetres of arc to the solid wall at its back.

There was a rattle of small gear following gravity and falling through from the head into the chest cavity. Inner circuitry shorted out with a crack and Cain twisted aside as an inspection plate on its chest ripped through the covering tunic and went into free flight followed by a jumble of colour coded leads. It made two jerky steps and pitched forward on its face with its motor developing a high pitched whine.

Cain used its own blaster drilling holes every few centimetres in the torso until the noise cut off.

White faced, Christie Maclean said 'That was horrible. It's like killing a human being. And you'd have done the same if it was one.'

It was unanswerable and he didn't try. The lodge had a massive wooden door and two small windows overlooking the gate. He burned out the lock and went inside.

Set up as a check point for freight movement, it had an operating console, a desk, a wall divided up into pigeon holes to file dockets and a large safe labelled in red BLASTING CHARGES.

Another mist cloud had settled over the valley and the gate was barely visible through the window, but as he switched power to the board and threw over a lever to a stop marked OPEN, he saw the whole structure including its support posts sink into the ground.

At the same time a siren began to wail from somewhere up the hill. Everybody liked to know when there was a gap in the perimeter.

Christie Maclean called, 'It's down. We can get across.'

'Out you go. Make for *The Oak*. I'll be right behind you.'

There could be a fail safe device that put the gate closed when there was a fault. So he withdrew to the door and fired into the console as he left.

Acrid blue smoke jetted from under its hood and the gate began to move. It was a metre out of its hole when he reached it and he took it like a hurdle.

It was a pity. It would have been useful to have it jammed open, but he reckoned that he had used his ration of luck for a fair spell and ran on through the mist to catch the girl.

As they approached *The Oak* the mist thinned again leaving only a steady rain. A dog began to bark from an outbuilding. Christie Maclean's hair was plastered in a dark copper skull cap and her sweater was moulded on like a skin.

Cain pressed the night bell and left his thumb on it for a count of ten.

There was a wait and he tried again. A window opened abruptly on the second floor and a man leaned out. High colour with a purplish tinge in the frank dawn light, grey hair standing up straight. They heard a woman's voice ask sharply, 'What is it Harry? What are you doing?'

Urbanity was not a round-the-clock service. The man said, 'Shut your cake hole. I'm trying to listen.'

'Listen to what for godsake?'

'How do I know until I hear it?'

Cain said, 'I have no wish to drive a wedge between a man and a woman. You have two travellers at your gate.'

'Do you know what time it is?'

'It's later than anybody thinks. Just do me a favour and open your door.'

'We've every room full. You can't stay here.'

The woman's voice said, 'Tell them we've every room full. They can't stay here.'

'I just did that, dumbhead.'

'Oh. What did they say?'

Cain said, 'Tell her that if you're not down in a count of ten, I'm coming in anyway.'

The head withdrew and there was the sound of feet making good time down a wooden stairway.

When the door opened Cain said, 'Thanks, bud. Show me where the video is. Bring two measures of Scotch and some eggs and bacon. Within the half hour we'll be on our way and you will have that good glow that comes from a fine deed.'

Beard matted and wet with rain, borrowed coat open to the navel, a heavy pistol in either pocket, Cain was no catch for the early morning. But an inn keeper learns flexibility. He also remembered he had an outside line from the kitchen. Public Safety could be along from Keswick City in ten minutes. He said 'There it is, through the arch. Help yourself. I'll go fix you something. It'll cost you a double service charge at this time.'

Cain handed Christie Maclean one of his pistols. 'Go with him Mac. Pick a fresh egg. Engage him in cheerful conversation.'

When they had gone he dialled an emergency number. He said 'Red star. Get me Fraser but quick. Cain.'

'He won't like that, Mr Cain.'

There was no picture, but he could imagine one of the trim special service staff sitting on her neat can in the relay station.

'You won't like it either if I come round there and beat your head in. Just do it.'

'All right. I'm only trying to be helpful. We've been trying to contact you. There's a signal for your recall.'

'I'll hear about it when I've talked to him.'

Fraser was ten seconds answering, 'Cain is it? I want you in. Right away. Stop whatever dumb thing you're doing. Is that clear?'

'Look, Chief. I want some action. Vort's place in Federal Park Three. A couple of military choppers with a task force. Vort's moved out of cover with a political bid that sounds fantastic. He's got Eisenberg and six Federal top brass in an underground complex. People like Glasman, General Quale and Fergus. Things are moving very fast. In a few days there won't be anything anybody can do about it.'

'That confirms it, Cain. You must be off of your head. I had Fergus himself round here not six hours ago. He'd had a report about you. You're a sick man. Where are you speaking from? I'll have you picked up.'

'That wasn't Fergus. They've put in android replacements.'

'Listen, Cain. I've known Harold Fergus for years. That was Fergus. Stay where you are. Don't do another thing. That's an order.'

Cain could imagine what was under way at the distant end. They would already have traced the call. Fraser would be using a second channel to get a posse started.

Fraser said, 'Are you still there?'

'I'm here. Okay. If that's the way you want it. I'll come and talk to you.'

'Just stay where you are.'

Cain switched out. So they had it sewn up. Fergus would pull all the strings needed to get him sequestered with a mental therapy unit and in a week he wouldn't believe it himself.

As he reached the lobby Christie Maclean showed up with mine host carrying a tray. He could stay and wait the ten minutes it would take for a fast Public Safety outfit to get out from Keswick City or he could make it a little harder for them by giving them a search in the mist.

He took a glass from the tray and emptied it. Maybe he ought to smash it in the rustic ingle, while his mind was still his own. But he replaced it and without looking at the girl said, 'Now hear this. I want you to take her through to a parlour and keep her out of the way. There'll be some visitors along for me. Tell them I made a call and then went out towards Vort's place. I'll meet them there. Don't mention Dr Maclean here. She shouldn't be involved. It's an official matter.'

Christie Maclean said, 'What are you doing Bob? What's happened?'

A fine act lost to the boards, he swung round to her with his face a prepared mask of frank regret, 'Look. You'll have to go along with this, Mac. Get a hire car and go back to Picton. I'll contact you as soon as I can. I have to meet a party from the department.'

He was expecting argument but she said, 'All right. I'll see you there then.' She held out the blaster by the barrel. 'You'd better have this. It makes me nervous.'

He thought that it was always so. The scene closed on a down beat. Only the hotelier looked pleased with more than half his trouble gone. He handed the tray to the girl and said, 'I'll see him out. Just go through and choose yourself a place, Doctor. You can stay as long as you like.'

She said 'I'll see you then,' and made her exit upstage, auburn ringlet drying out and regaining some of its elasticity, carrying her tray with a straight back. A domestic note to end on.

They were a pace from the door when the bell rang.

Cain said 'Open it,' and stepped out of sight. That was a record beater even for a department that prided itself on moving fast. But the voice that spoke from the mist had no official ring about it. 'I saw your light, Whack. I'm lookin' for a research outfit. Name of Vort. The chart says I'm right at it, but there's nothin' to see in this mist.'

'Your chart's right, son. Two hundred metres. Keep down to the surface road and you can't miss it. On the left.'

Cain signalled for him to leave the door open and was through as the caller reached the dim shape of a long shuttle. The pilot climbed in and there was a whine of gear as he lowered the six wheel bogie and retracted his landing skids.

Cain approached from the tail end as the skids went flat in their housing. Through the plexiglass dome he could see Langton's burly figure, head and shoulders over a squab. It was familiar and he knew he had seen it on department files, but it was not until he had swung himself under the chassis and was hanging under the car with his feet hooked in two bracing struts that recall clicked.

So Southern Hem were sending a top man. They would not get much change out of Vort. But that was no comfort. One way or another he had to work something out. Something that would force Fraser's hand and bring Vort into the open.

By the time the shuttle reached the gatehouse, he had a rough draft and was thinking himself into a state of concentration that would shut out every other side issue and give him an overriding programme.

Cain saw the cattle grid slide past ten centimetres from his back and reckoned he was lucky there was no upstanding centre stop to hold a double leaf door. The car was taking it slowly with its main beams throwing the mist into a white fuzz and the pilot taking his course from the UHF scanner.

Well placed to pick up a change in motion Cain dropped clear as soon as he felt the driving wheels bite and rolled smartly on his stomach ready to shoot at anything moving from the lodge.

But the mist was hanging thickly around the arch and he padded off after the car.

At the down slope to the cluster of reception buildings, he struck off right and met the dry stone wall that marked the edge of the beck. Beyond it, he found a three metre drop to the river bed, littered with water smoothed boulders.

He was banking that there would be no intervening fence between the two parts of Vort's property and when he had climbed the slope he found he was right.

There was a narrow path along the crest of the hill and he took it, moving left across the frontage of the reception area.

At the end of the line, he met the fence and followed it down until he was above the lodge and the quarry access road.

The mist was sticking in patches, but the gate and the check point were clear. Somebody had moved the android. The door was half open.

He dropped to the roadway and went for the door at a run with a blaster in either hand, kicked it wide and let momentum carry him in.

It was empty. The console was a charred wreck. They would be intending to put in a replacement unit.

He set a laser for a shallow cutting beam and sliced out the hinge side of the blasting charge locker.

It was stacked up with gun metal tubes and an array of clock detonators.

Cain worked like a machine using lengths of cable from the shattered console, tying the charges in bundles of six until he had four bombs, fitting a setting dial to each. He found a khaki drill coverall behind the door, put it on instead of his white coat and used the coat to make a rough sack.

Finally he wired up the rest of the stock and put a timer on set to go in ten minutes.

Cain went up the ridge with his sack on his shoulder and backtracked to a point above the reception area. He could see down into the courtyard. He fished out a bomb. Set it for ten minutes on and lobbed it to fall in the parking lot where four shuttles including Langton's and the mobile lab were drawn up. Then he went straight for the ventilation shaft.

It was clear. Even androids would not search for people who had already gone. They had also picked up the headless sentry.

He checked the knots on his bundle and began to go down.

At the bottom he took the duct opposite the one they had used before on a hunch that the corridor to the politicos' ward lay that way.

Second along there was an identical set up and he thought he was there, but the figures in bed were different and along at the far end there was a black one.

Nothing much was going on. The android counterparts wherever they were would be feigning sleep or recharging their motors. The operating consoles were not manned and a guard with a carbine on a sling was pacing the mid floor.

He came down, passed out of sight and reappeared walking the other way. Cain shoved out the holding clips and held the cover ready to drop.

The android turned and came back. As his head went out of vision Cain threw the screen to fall behind it and as it spun round to check it out, he was leaning out of his hole firing point blank in a long burst from the back of the head to the middle of the trunk.

It was still deciding which way to fall when Cain caught it and lowered it to the deck.

Delacroix was awake straining at clamps which fixed him by wrists and ankles to his tilted bed.

Cain shifted the head gear and then began to throw switches. 'Listen. Get along the row and rouse them all out. Take them up through that shaft. There's a way to the top. A long climb but get moving.'

Brigitta Ross, next off the circuit said, 'I'd like to find my pants before I start climbing any ladders.'

Delacroix said, 'Where's your priority? Don't answer. Just move. If you go first, it'll encourage those below.'

They were a bemused crew but biddable and went into the duct as though still following deep hypnotic suggestion.

Cain opened a panel under the long computer spread and dropped in one of his charges on a fifteen minute fuse.

Delacroix had waited for him in the duct and the tail end Charley was already in the shaft. He said 'What next Bob? Anything I can do? I'd like to even the score a little.'

Cain gave him a blaster. 'This way. We have to get another party out.'

The VIP operations theatre was two outlets along and work was still going on. Six operators manned the consoles and there was a guard standing four square at the end of the row.

Cain fixed the scene in his mind and said 'Give me cover.'

He shoved away the clips, threw the grating clear and was shooting before it hit the deck.

He saw the trace line biting home and was through the gap with the guard struggling to bring its carbine into aim.

There was another hidden by the angle and he knew as he fired again that his luck had run out. He felt the impact in his left shoulder and was slewed round by the force. Then Delacroix was raking the android with a burst and it pitched forward to the deck.

One operator left his seat and ran for the door. Delacroix fired again and there was a wholly human scream.

It discouraged the rest. They sat tight hands on the counter, heads twisted round to watch the action.

Working one handed, Cain had Eisenberg free.

He said thickly, 'I don't know how much you know or guess, but this is no place to be. Get your friends out of here. Move it along or there'll be seven vacancies in the government.'

In his lucid intervals, Eisenberg had found time to think. He recognized the truth when he saw it.

Cain left them to work it out. He found a dispensary and rounded up the operating team. When they were in, Delacroix was already shoving the last Minister into the duct.

'What now?'

'Hand out that bag.'

'Can you manage?'

'I can manage. Get them all up top. There's a road past the quarry. In ten minutes there'll be a gap blown in the fence. Take them through.'

'What about you?'

'I'll be along.'

He opened a maintenance panel in the computer

spread and set another charge with twelve minutes on its clock.

Climbing into the duct was heavy work and he had to take a spell before he could go on. There was one charge remaining and he wanted Vort to have it for himself.

Three ventilators along, he was sidetracked by the view. He was looking into the mechanical heart of the complex.

It was a circular pit on a fifty metre diameter with a raised inspection way all round and sophisticated hardware close packed on the floor of the well.

It was all there. A power plant to make the complex independent of the Federal grid, control panels for outgoing signals to keep the android agents full of sap, the ice berg tip of a reactor with its mass sunk in the living rock.

Still programmed to find Vort, he moved on with the end of the duct only thirty metres away.

The last ventilator was the pay off and he looked through in disbelief thinking that he was finally moving into hallucination.

It was a small room. More like a family vault. In the centre was a catafalque built of green slate slabs. Lying on it under a plexiglass dome, arms crossed on his chest was an emaciated figure.

The face was just recognizable. It was Vort himself, waiting for resurrection.

In a moment of absolute clarity Cain saw how it was. Vort had succeeded too well. The top hand was his own *doppleganger*, an android gone solo. The Vorticists themselves were neatly outflanked. The ultimate programme was not for any human system whatever, it was for an android takeover.

It was a nice ironic twist.

He sat back on his heels and thought about it. Did it matter so much? If the human crop was phased out and self perpetuating mechanicals moved over the set where would the difference lie? An observer from outside would see the same overall pattern. Figures moving over the canvas busy keeping themselves in being, fashioning new parts, creating power, consuming, meeting problems with rational thought that they had inherited from the species they had replaced.

It could even be a logical development. The food chain for biological man was under constant strain and must eventually break down. Sooner or later the planet would not support life as they knew it. Why not hand on to a mechanical mind which could carry the thinking eye around in an asbestos socket over a wilderness of pumice?

But not yet. They hadn't finished with it yet.

The head on the slab moved and the face turned to look straight at the ventilator.

Cain slapped open the clips and dropped through. A faint voice whispered as though speaking straight into his head, 'You are right. I have had all the time in the world to think about it. You are certainly right.'

There was a handle to lift and the dome hinged away. He helped Vort off his slab and the man was bird light, all skin and bone.

Vort said, 'I know what you have in mind. I ask you to let me do it. No-one has a better right. What I created I should destroy.'

Cain thought he had a point, but it was no time to be sentimental. Any mortician would be wheeling in a casket believing sincerely that it was overdue.

But there was nothing wrong with Vort's mind. All his vitality seemed to have concentrated in his head and sharpened his ESP.

'I can do it. I *have* to do it. You must give me this chance. This is what human judgement is about in the last analysis. We can fall into error, but finally we know what is right and what is wrong. Give me your bomb and open the door.'

Cain came to a decision. There was a pattern in it. In Vort's place he would want it for himself. He reached into the duct and brought out the last charge. He said 'Set the pointer to zero and you have about five seconds.'

'Open the door.'

Cain burned out the lock and found Vort at his elbow breathing deeply like a gaunt fakir, carrying his bomb like a ceremonial cushion.

'Good luck, then.'

'And to you, young man. Now go.'

It was easier said than done. When he reached the duct a wave of vertigo held him on his knees for a long count and the tunnel was opening and closing like a long throat.

When he moved he had no idea how long he had been.

At the power centre he stopped again, with the scene in a haze. When it settled, there was a change. Almost opposite, Vort and Langton were on the gallery with a couple of guards. He was giving the Southern Hem rep a conducted tour.

Cain thought he had been a fool. He should have known the old man would never get through. He ought to have finished it himself.

At least he could neutralize the android.

Forcing himself to concentrate he chocked his right wrist on his knee for the aim.

Then Langton was pointing to something out of sight on the near side of the gallery and the Vort android was shouting to the guards. They moved left and right round the gallery at a fast clip. A grey bundle sailed into view in an arc that would drop it neatly on the reactor housing.

An adrenalin boost kicked Cain into movement. Head down, he went at a stumbling run along the duct.

He was counting and got to ten as he reached the bottom of the ventilation shaft.

The floor rocked under his feet and a hurricane wind from the duct caught him and carried him to the far side.

Cain set himself to go on. Heaving himself a rung at a time. Swaying out over the drop when the vertigo swept through his head. An android programmed to crawl out of a hole until it fell apart.

There was a second hammer thud from below and a gust that blew small trash up the chimney like so much shrapnel.

If he had been on an open section he would have been swept from his hold, but he was hooked on a platform and felt the debris smash into its inside.

That would be the charge in the first ward. Another would be due any time at all. He made the next platform and waited, then the next and heard the thud of the third bomb.

The whole shaft was in a quiver. As soon as the blast roared through, he was climbing again. Much slower now, heaving himself painfully from rung to rung with the sure knowledge that the time was very near when no amount of will would shift him to the next.

Either his mind was finally blown or he was climbing into a brilliant light. Hooking his arm through a rung, he stopped to consider it. Elongated shadows were reaching down the tube. There was a tightness round his chest and a free floating face not half a metre off. Then the scene blacked and he knew he had let go his holdfast, but contrary to all expectation he was falling slowly and, if sense could be believed, was falling up the shaft in defiance of Newton's apple.

Christie Maclean's voice was saying insistently, 'Bob, you've got to wake up. You've got to say what's happening down there.'

She had an arm under his shoulders and he heaved himself up. He was on the high ground above the quarry. A pillar of smoke and flame was going up from the reception area and the whole perimeter round the lodge was in a state of smash. There was a whole raft of people round about and an Actualizer crew had gotten in on the act with a mobile broadcast unit.

Another voice spoke into his left ear. Billot was there, face streaked with carbon. He said, 'I was called to the Polytech and found the android got up as your friend Delacroix. So I came right on up here. Dr Maclean persuaded me to follow you in and the fence conveniently blew a hole in itself. I reckon, mind you, that it was a public danger. Now, granting you credibility for the sake of argument what does go on down below?'

Cain said, 'Get everybody out. There's a reactor with damaged control gear. Evacuate the village.'

The man with the camera said reverently, 'Holy Cow. If anybody had told me there was anything to follow the seven burghers walking out of that hole stark naked I wouldn't have believed it. And that black one with the lush dark number on his back. But a real old fashioned nuclear blow-out might just do it. Quick Gary, start pulling out. I want us set up on that hillside. I'll get a diamond award for this.'

Cain said wearily, 'Posthumous, but don't let it worry you.'

Christie Maclean said, 'That's all you can have Lieutenant, I'm giving him a shot whether you like it or not.'

Billot said 'Okay Doctor. He's all yours. Everybody out. Move it along. At the double.'

There was an orderly stampede to a line of cars drawn up on the quarry road; three with the Keswick City Public Safety emblem and Billot's with its rampant Dolphin on a stylized sea.

He stopped to confer with his opposite number. 'You're the local fuzz, Jack. Winkle that crowd out of *The Oak* and evacuate the village. Maybe they've been fixed up with a blanket apiece. Two kilometres okay?'

'With the anti-rad screens that should be plenty. What

are you doing with Cain? I had it on a top docket to take him in.'

'I'll hold him. As he is he can't get far. Okay?'

'Okay.'

It was early in the morning for a wide public and the Actualities man was limited with his one camera. But those who had switched on to see what grief there was about as a starter for the new day were held to their screens.

He did his best, catching the VIP column in a second move from *The Oak* still bemused like a rounded up orgy, panning over the valley with long shots of the quarry and the burning car lot. Even a military chopper, late on the scene and circling while its commander talked to Billot.

It was a dialogue that Billot reckoned would only come his way once in a lifetime and he made the most of it.

The operator said, 'Believe it or not Chief, there's a monkey on the blower who says he's Harry Fergus. Public Safety Number One.'

There was a face on the video to prove it. Fresher looking than the one Billot had just seen and all ready to be nasty. It said, 'What's going on, Officer? I remind you that you're on private property. You could lose your rank for this.'

Billot said, 'I'll worry about that Harry. Now you have a whole lot of other things to worry about. Don't get your cogs in a spin. Commissioner Fergus is back in circulation. You can land now and give yourself up as an exhibit for the Public Safety Museum or I'll call for an interceptor to shoot you down.'

The screen blanked and the chopper dropped for the quarry in a tight turn.

The network got it all. Cars drawn up in a fold of the hill; valley gone still as death; a man made Krakatoa opening up and the chopper shot vertical like a flung stone. Then a sliding rumble and the whole complex, copse, houses, fence, quarry were all gone and the beck was arching out in a rainbow fall into a vast pothole.

Cain got himself up to date on an evening newscast. Decontamination teams were thick on the ground and *The Oak* was fifty metres from the lip of a brand new tourist attraction which would be a money spinner when the area was given a clearance.

He had seen a succession of visitors. Keswick City General had given him a small private ward and it was filling up with grapes and flowers.

But the one he wanted to see had not shown up.

Left side heavily strapped he roamed about the room unable to settle. They said he could go in forty-eight hours, but he reckoned he would be ready for psychiatric treatment by that time.

He went out on the balcony overlooking the courtyard and watched the flow of people in and out. They could be androids at that. And for the most part it wouldn't matter a damn.

A door opened at his back and he went in to see who it was. Fraser himself was due anytime for a de-briefing and he had already decided that he had had enough. He would finish the course at Picton and work out a new line.

She was standing just inside the door as though unsure of welcome, very trim in a cyclamen tabard, hair combed into an elastic bell, eyes still dark with strain almost all pupil.

Making conversation she said, 'I wasn't sure whether you'd want to pick up Picton contacts. Mission completed, agents melt into cover don't they?'

'What gave you that idea?'

'I'm an avid reader.'

The gap had narrowed to half a metre and she had no room to manoeuvre.

'You haven't read the right book,'

He was near enough to put a hand on her shoulder.

Human contact and human chemistry. It would be a long time, if ever, before android simulation could copy that. Biological man had the edge.

And biological woman. Helping the handicapped in the best tradition of her craft, Christie Maclean linked her fingers behind his head to push a good thing along.

For Cain it was a home coming he had not expected to have. He knew what he would say to Fraser. There were all kinds of complications ahead, but as of now only one issue of any importance and it was settled already at a level not tapped by speech.